THE
WONDROUS
PRUNE

THE WONDROUS PRUNE

ELLIE CLEMENTS

BLOOMSBURY
CHILDREN'S BOOKS
LONDON OXFORD NEW YORK NEW DELHI SYDNEY

BLOOMSBURY CHILDREN'S BOOKS
Bloomsbury Publishing Plc
50 Bedford Square, London WC1B 3DP, UK
29 Earlsfort Terrace, Dublin 2, Ireland

BLOOMSBURY, BLOOMSBURY CHILDREN'S BOOKS and the Diana
logo are trademarks of Bloomsbury Publishing Plc

First published in Great Britain in 2022 by Bloomsbury Publishing Plc

A catalogue record for this book is available from the British Library

ISBN: PB: 978-1-5266-3832-8; eBook: 978-1-5266-3833-5

2 4 6 8 10 9 7 5 3 1

Typeset by RefineCatch Limited, Bungay, Suffolk

Printed and bound in Great Britain by CPI Group (UK) Ltd, Croydon CR0 4YY

To find out more about our authors and books visit www.bloomsbury.com
and sign up for our newsletters

For Mum
You'll forever be in my heart

CHAPTER 1

Has something completely astounding and spectacular but also totally surprising ever happened to you? My name is Prune Melinda Robinson. I'm eleven years old, and something like that has just happened to me. Something so extraordinary, so out of this world, I'm still amazed by it now! And I bet you will be too.

I'll never forget the day my life changed forever ...

It all started one Sunday. It was a perfectly ordinary day, well, so I thought: I ate my lunch as usual and went back upstairs to my room. But then, as I went and sat down on my bed, I was suddenly surrounded by the most amazing colours all bunched together like clouds.

Magenta, coral, teal, lavender, and so many shades of yellow – the colour of sweet lemonade, sunflowers and cheese on toast – plus reds, which were redder than the tastiest strawberries and my mama's favourite lipstick. Not only that, but amongst the colour clouds were the greenest greens and the brownest browns, the pinkest pinks and blues the colour of lagoons, and not forgetting my favourite colour of all, orange, which shone as beautiful as a sunrise.

I pinched myself and rubbed my eyes to make sure I wasn't dreaming because it was as if I'd been transported to the most magnificent and enchanting place, my bedroom feeling like a forest of endless bloom. Though, when I reached out to touch the colours, I couldn't feel a thing.

The colours were all so bright – brighter than the sky and even brighter than the moon when it gets all big and fat and sits outside your window like it wants to move in.

They were even brighter than my grandpa's smile, and no one had a smile quite as bright as Poppa B. Well, no one except Grandma Jean. Her smile was more brilliant than the ruby earrings she liked to wear, a gift from Poppa after they got married. She wore them to his funeral – her earrings and her smile the only things that were cheerful on that bleak November day.

Some people didn't get why my grandma looked so happy when they were crying and wailing, even those that didn't know my poppa but had only turned up because they'd heard Mama was making her famous potato salad for the wake. That's what my brother Jesse told me anyway.

But Grandma Jean said she had already cried all the tears she had when Poppa first got sick, and when the cancer began to make him weaker and smaller until it finally took away that beautiful bright smile of his. So when he died, Grandma made sure smiling was all she did because even though she was sad, most of all she was just grateful that Poppa wasn't suffering any more.

And now Grandma's gone too. She died two and a half months ago and I've been missing her heaps. Sometimes I get so sad that it feels like I have a shattered plate where my heart should be that no amount of superglue can put back together.

There was so much already that had changed in my life before the bizarre events of that day, and trying to get used to a world without Grandma had been the biggest change of all. To add to all this, I was about to start a new school the next day, *and* we'd just moved to a new house. Well, it was actually the house that had belonged to Grandma and Poppa B in a town called Delmere. A place where people say nothing interesting ever happens.

That was until that Sunday, when *everything* changed.

CHAPTER 2

'Prune!' my brother called from his bedroom, which is adjacent to mine. 'I've got a present for you. Prune!'

At the sound of his voice, the colours started to fade, shrinking like dots until there were just a few hanging above my head like a sparkly crown.

'What present?' I called back curiously, forgetting my worries about starting my new school the next morning and how strange it felt to be in this house without Grandma Jean.

'Come and take a look!' he said.

I went into Jesse's room to find him standing on his bed, replacing a picture of a meadow with a poster of his favourite basketball player, Titus Reid. He'd not long started unpacking his boxes, whereas I'd unpacked all my things when we moved in two days earlier. Although Jesse's room is bigger than mine, it most definitely isn't as nice. Everything is grey. Grey wallpaper, grey rug, grey curtains.

My room might be the smallest, but to me, it's the best room in the house. It used to be Grandma and Poppa's guest room, and it has these sweet little ornaments that include a set of dancing ballerinas and a lamp that's shaped like a tortoise. I could've put them in the cellar where we'd put most of Grandma Jean's things, but they were all so lovely I decided to keep them. Before we moved, Jesse and I used to share a room, so it was great to finally have a bedroom all to myself, especially as Jesse has a habit of farting *a lot*.

A long time ago, Jesse's room belonged to Mama. On the wall, it still has the tiny marks she drew to track her height when she was a young girl. The lines only go up a little way because Mama is quite short. I am already nearly as tall as her, and she thinks I'll soon grow past her just like Jesse has. He's fifteen and is close to six feet, but I'd never want to grow that tall. I'd just like to be medium-sized – a height that's halfway between Mama and Jesse.

'Here's your present,' said Jesse, handing me the picture of the meadow. 'I was going to put it with Grandma's stuff, but then I thought you might like it.'

'Thanks.' I smiled, taking a closer look at the picture. It was actually quite pretty and had been painted with watercolours. I knew this because art is one of my favourite things in the whole world, and you'll never catch me without my sketchbook. I love drawing just as much as I love superhero films, mint-scented bath bombs, red velvet cupcakes, chocolate ice cream and my butterfly hair clips that look like real butterflies.

I'm actually an award-winning artist, having come second place at my old school's annual art competition a few months back. It was for my picture of a dolphin doing an aerial somersault. Plus I came third in a big inter-school competition with my picture of Spider-Man web-swinging through New York City. My favourite picture ever is a portrait I did of Grandma, even though I didn't win an award for it. I was only seven when I drew it, and my drawing has improved a lot since then, but I still feel so proud because I know how much Grandma loved it.

It still amazes me how I got her to sit still for a whole hour and she didn't fidget once; not like Jesse when I tried to do his portrait. He could barely sit still for two minutes, let alone an hour. Hopefully, when I grow up and become a famous artist, I'll get to draw lots of people's portraits, including my favourite singer, Keirra Grace.

As I looked at the painting Jesse gave me, I knew I still had a long way to go before my pictures would be anywhere near as good. I'd love to live near a meadow. As far as I know, there aren't any meadows in Delmere, and there certainly weren't any meadows where we used to live – a neighbouring town called Ocean View. But it didn't exactly have an ocean either, or a lake or a river, and the only views I ever got were of the bins at the back of our old tower block. We did have Shellwood Park though, which had a basketball court and a playground, only Mama didn't like us going there because some local boys, or 'hooligans' as she preferred to call them, saw the park as theirs. Sometimes they'd even try and charge people to go in. One boy wanted Mama to pay him a pound when we went to have a picnic there one Saturday.

Mama told him, 'I don't know what you think you're doing, but you need to get out of my way right now, young man. And if you think you're getting a single penny out of me, you can think again!'

She tried to push open the gate, but the boy pushed it back, stopping us from going in. So, in the end, we had our picnic at home on the living room carpet.

'At least when we move, I won't have to keep fretting about you hanging around those hooligans,' Mama said to Jesse while we ate. 'And nor will I have to worry that you'll end up in some young offenders institution,' she added.

But Jesse just laughed and told Mama that she was overreacting.

'My friends aren't hooligans, Mama. And why worry? Nothing bad is going to happen to me.'

But his response made Mama extra cross.

'I worry because you're my son, Jesse,' she said, her voice as firm as it gets. 'And I'll never stop worrying, even when you're a man in his fifties, and please stop laughing because none of this is funny.'

But that's just my brother. He never takes things seriously and thinks he's so smart when he still can't even solve my Rubik's cube. I've been solving it since I was eight! But there are some things Jesse's good at. He makes the most brilliant strawberry milkshakes and I suppose he's not half bad at telling a funny joke or two. Yet the problem with Jesse is that he just can't seem to understand that it's not smart to bunk off school, which he's done *a lot*.

You'd think he'd also know that if you're going to steal something from a shop, you'd better be prepared to get caught. But no, not Jesse. Not even after he got caught red-handed trying to steal chocolate from Thorne's Express. That's when I decided my brother must have his brain missing – why else would he be so stupid?

It wasn't the first time Jesse had stolen something either. He was really lucky the shop's owner, Mr Thorne, didn't call the police. But he did call Mama, who was furious, and it was only when she threatened to call the police on Jesse herself that my brother admitted that his friend Bryce had dared him to do it.

'So if Bryce Mackenzie dared you to jump off a bridge, would you do that too?' asked Mama when he returned home.

But Jesse just kept his head bowed, saying nothing.

'That's why Bryce and the rest of those *so-called friends* of yours aren't really your friends at all – not when they're busy trying to get you into trouble,' said Mama. 'And that had better be the last time I hear you've stolen something. You've got me feeling so ashamed, Jesse!'

Then she started to cry and I stared at Jesse long and hard as I hated seeing Mama cry.

But as I looked at him across the living room, I wondered if he had a heart missing too, because it was like he just didn't care. Not one bit.

'Stop staring, Pugface!' He scowled at me.

Pugface is a name Jesse calls me when he wants to be horrible. But it's only because he knows his name isn't as sweet as mine.

'But why would anyone want a dozy name like *Prune*?' he once said when I told him he was jealous. 'And Mama's just as dozy naming you after some ugly bugly fruit that makes people want to do number twos!'

Not that Jesse would dare say that to Mama's face. But anyway, I don't care what he thinks of my name because I love it, hugely. Plus I happen to think prunes are super delicious.

Jesse's been friends with Bryce since he was eleven, ever since Bryce beat up a boy who was picking on him. After that he became my brother's hero, replacing Poppa B, who'd been a hero to us both. Bryce used to go to Jesse's old school – well, that was until he got permanently excluded for constantly bunking off. But for some reason, Jesse still looks up to Bryce, or at least acts as though he owes him something. I reckon it's because he thinks Bryce is somehow living some ultra-cool life just because he's seventeen and has his own car and got his dad to convert their garage into a gym. His family have lots of money, but Bryce likes to steal and walks around acting like he's as hard as Iron Man. I only wish Jesse could see that Bryce isn't someone worth getting into trouble for.

'Earth to Prune, hello!' Jesse droned through a rolled-up poster, snapping me out of my thoughts. 'You've got the picture, so you can go now.'

'Jesse, can you see these colours?' I said, pointing above my head where the dots had been.

'Huh? What colours?'

I looked up and then went over to his mirror to double-check. The colours had now completely vanished. But just where had they come from? Or had it simply been my eyes playing tricks on me?

CHAPTER 3

As I looked at my reflection in Jesse's mirror, I remembered that Grandma Jean said she used to see dots and squiggles in front of her eyes and that's why she wore glasses – to make the dots less dotty and the squiggles less squiggly.

So, what was going on?

'Instead of admiring yourself in my mirror, why don't you make yourself useful and help me unpack?' said Jesse.

I turned round. 'Jesse, do you think I need glasses?'

'Do I look like an optician? How would I know?' he replied, sticking another poster of Titus Reid to the wall.

Pushing a box out of the way, I went and sat over at Jesse's desk. 'I think my eyes are going funny.'

'You mean like this,' said Jesse, looking at me with his eyes crossed and his tongue out to one side.

I giggled but then blew out my cheeks.

'I'm being serious, Jesse. I think I might need glasses.'

'In that case, when Mama gets back from the shops, why don't you ask her if she'll let you go and get your eyes checked out? I'm sure there must be a couple of opticians in this town.'

'And do you reckon they'll be able to explain what I saw?' I'd described to Jesse what had happened in my bedroom, reeling off a list of some of the colours I'd seen, but his expression remained baffled.

'Are you sure it was *colours*?' my brother replied. 'Hey, it wasn't a ghost was it? Because as much as I loved Grandma and Poppa B, no way do I want to live in a haunted house. It's bad enough we had to move to this rubbish town.'

'No, I didn't see a ghost,' I said, but with a shudder.

A ghost was the *last* thing I wanted to see – not that I thought our grandparents would ever try to haunt us. Still, I decided there and then that perhaps it was best I slept with the lamp on that night, just in case.

'So you didn't see any colours above my head when I came in?' I asked.

'No. You've already asked me that! You're really not making any sense right now, Prune.'

'But they were there – I'm sure of it – and they were in my room.'

'What?'

'The colours.'

'What colours?' said Jesse huffily.

'The ones I've been telling you all about!' I was getting frustrated now.

'All right, let me get this straight. Are you saying you saw something that's not really there?' asked Jesse.

I shrugged, feeling deflated.

'Look, Prune, this isn't some house out of a fairy story, you know, where mysterious things happen. So you either saw a ghost or you didn't.'

'It wasn't a ghost,' I said.

'Well, that's good then,' Jesse replied, making me wish I hadn't asked.

But his words did get me thinking.

What if our house really was the kind of house you get in a fairytale? The kind that is never quite as it seems. The kind that is magical. And this very thought had my tummy skipping with excitement, because nothing would be more amazing than getting to live in a house full of magic. So as I left Jesse's room, I decided that I'd do a bit of investigating. I'd start with the cellar because, if there really was a magical force within the house, then maybe it was down there, nestled amongst Grandma and Poppa B's things.

All I needed to do was find it.

CHAPTER 4

Closing Jesse's door gently behind me, I found myself wishing my grandma was still alive so I could ask her if the house was magic or not. It still feels weird that her house is now ours. When we moved in, I half expected to see her standing at the door, waiting to greet us. But all that was waiting for us was a big, silent house. A house that I had now decided to investigate.

I made my way down to the cellar. It was chock full of boxes containing Grandma Jean and Poppa B's stuff, but there were no colour clouds to be found anywhere. I was hoping that they'd perhaps burst out of one of the boxes, but the only thing that burst was the button on a cardigan that I tried on. I think it might've been Mama's when she was my age. I thought the cardigan would fit, but it was way too small.

I looked in my grandparents' old wardrobe to see if the colour clouds were hiding in there, but the only things inside were a couple of clothes hangers and a broken umbrella. And when I checked behind the wardrobe, the only clouds I was met with were clouds of dust. My investigation had hit a brick wall, literally. But there was still one person I could ask if this house was magical – Mama. After all, she had grown up here, so if anyone should know, it would be her.

Until that day I'd never seen any colour clouds in the house, and there certainly weren't any when me, Mama and Jesse used to visit. I always loved coming over. On warm days we'd all sit in the garden drinking Grandma's homemade lemonade as she'd tell us the story of how she and Poppa first met. She'd just moved over from America and was working in a library, and Poppa had come in to return a book that was a year overdue. Grandma gave him a piece of her mind because it was a book lots of people had been waiting to read. Poppa responded by asking her out on a date, and Grandma found herself saying yes.

No matter how many times she'd tell me this story, I always enjoyed hearing it. I also loved helping Grandma make her favourite dessert, peach cobbler, while her and

Poppa's soul music records played in the background on their old record player.

There is so much I miss about Grandma Jean, from the way her eyes would dance whenever she talked about Poppa to the nickname she gave me – Prunebear. And I miss her hugs, which always felt as warm as her American biscuits straight from the oven. I miss seeing her smooth brown hands (not like a grandma's hands at all) knitting, stitching, gardening, baking – because Grandma always had to be doing something. She'd say it was because she liked to keep herself busy.

Grandma Jean died in her sleep – peacefully, according to Mama. Grandma's sister, Auntie Carol, told me that's one of the best ways to die, and it was something I thought about a lot in the days leading up to Grandma's funeral, because how could there be a *best way* to die when you're no longer around the people you love or able to do the things you enjoy? And it could just be simple things like listening to the birds chirping in the morning or feeling the crunch of snow beneath your feet. I only hope I get to live to the age Grandma was, or older, so I can enjoy the things I love and any new things I might come to love for as long as possible.

I pushed the wardrobe back against the wall and, just as I was about to walk out of the cellar, something caught my eye. It was the colour clouds – out of nowhere, they began to bloom around me.

Have they just been hiding? I wondered.

I wasn't sure where though, considering I had checked every box. But seeing the colours again did at least cheer me up. It was just a shame they didn't stick around for long. They faded away after only a few minutes. Yet the question remained: how did they get there? But I guessed only Mama would be able to answer that question.

'So are you excited about starting your new school tomorrow?' asked Mama later that afternoon as she was braiding my hair.

'No, not really,' I admitted, looking up at her as I sat on the carpet.

'Oh, are you feeling nervous?' said Mama.

'Yeah, a little,' I replied, even though the only thing on my mind was where the colours might have come from.

Would I even get to see them again?

'Well, I suppose that's to be expected,' said Mama, parting a section of my hair with the comb. 'After all, everything is going to be new – new teachers, new class-mates, new uniform.'

But having Mama remind me of all these new things almost had me worrying again. Much as I'd been glad to leave Ocean View, as it meant Jesse would finally be away from Bryce and his other mates, part of me wished I could've stayed at my old school, Oak Nolan. I only had a couple of months left of Year Six, so it didn't make much sense having to leave, plus I was missing my best friend Corinne terribly. We'd been friends since Reception when we used to try to convince everyone we were twins. I was even missing my old teacher Mrs Hart, even though she could be a little grumpy sometimes.

'What if I don't make any friends, Mama?' I said, looking up at her again.

'Oh, you will, sweetheart, and I'm sure Maple Lane will be just fine. But it is perfectly normal you know to be nervous, and sometimes it can take a little while to get used to a new place.' She patted my shoulder. 'But I bet you by the end of the week, you'll be telling me how much you like it there.'

'Mama, do you think this house might be magical?' I said to her suddenly.

'Magical?' she repeated. 'Well, interesting you say that because when I was a kid, I used to pretend I was a princess and this house was a magical castle.' She giggled. 'Though, one thing I can say *was* magical was the speed at which your grandma's peach cobbler would always disappear any time we had visitors. But it did taste sublime, so I'm not surprised.'

'But did you ever see any strange colours?'

'*Strange colours?* Um, I'm not sure what you mean – there's nothing I've ever seen here that I'd say was strange. Why? Have you seen something?'

'I thought I did earlier, but I'm sure it was nothing,' I found myself saying quickly, feeling even more puzzled. 'I guess it would just be nice if this house was magical and could feel as special as when Grandma and Poppa lived here.'

'Oh, it will feel special, Prune, I promise you. I'll make it a home we can all be happy in for many years to come,' said Mama. 'And I've just thought of something.'

'What?'

'Something that I know will brighten your day.'

Mama then left the room, returning a few minutes later carrying a brown leather rucksack.

'It was in the cellar amongst your grandma's things. It belonged to me when I was your age,' she said, handing it to me. 'You did mention that you wanted a new rucksack. I hope you don't mind that it's an old one I'm giving you.'

'No, Mama, not at all. I love it,' I said, smiling gratefully.

Despite a few marks and a slight musty smell, the rucksack was lovely.

'I knew you'd like it,' said Mama, looking pleased.

And she was right. The rucksack did cheer me up, plus it was nice to think I'd be carrying something around with me that had meant so much to Mama. Maybe it'd even bring me some good luck for my first day, and I was happy to see that it was big enough to fit my sketchbook.

After Mama had finished braiding my hair, I took my rucksack up to my room. I was desperate to see the colours again, but for the rest of the day not one colour cloud appeared and this made me wonder if it'd all just been my imagination.

Maybe there were no real colour clouds at all.

CHAPTER 5

'You do know, Mama, I can find my own way to school,' said Jesse as we ate breakfast the following day.

It was Monday morning, our first day at our new schools, and Jesse was acting like he was too old to have Mama drop him off at the gate.

She was planning on dropping us off before making her way to work. She'd recently started a new job in Delmere as a waitress at a pizza restaurant called Big Sal's, which did pizzas as huge as a hula hoop.

'I can easily walk, save you being late for work,' said Jesse, stretching for the carton of orange juice that was on the table.

'Careful!' I hissed, as he almost knocked it on to the picture I was drawing in my sketchbook of Groot

22

from *Guardians of the Galaxy*.

'No – I said I'd take you to school, so that's what I'm going to do. In any case, I already told Sal I'd be in late,' said Mama, taking a sip of her coffee. Then, putting down the cup, she looked at my brother intently. 'I want you to promise me, Jesse, that you won't start skipping school again and that you'll try your hardest to do well.'

'I promise, Mama,' said Jesse, but his face looked like he wasn't promising a thing.

And it was obvious Mama wasn't convinced either as she let out a sigh.

'Sometimes, boy, I don't know what I have to do to get through to you.'

She looked at me. 'For pity's sake, Prune, will you just finish your cereal and stop drawing.'

Jesse had obviously put Mama in a bad mood because she didn't normally mind me drawing pictures at breakfast.

'Why do you hate school so much?' I asked Jesse when Mama had left the kitchen.

'It's just dull,' he responded plainly.

'But you know Mama says that if you want to get a good job, then you need to get a good education.'

'Yeah, but who's to say I won't become a famous basketball player. Bryce reckons I could make millions. So what would I need school for?'

'You need it because it's important, Jesse. Anyway, what does Bryce know when he got kicked out of school?'

'He knows a lot actually – like how you should never miss a good opportunity when you see one. He didn't miss the opportunity of making sure his dad got him Titus Reid's autograph when his dad met him on a business trip to LA. But once I get scouted, that'll be the start of my basketball career and me becoming mega wealthy. And like Bryce, my house will have its own gym and maybe I'll even have a cinema room.' Jesse pushed his chair back. 'Like Poppa B used to say, *You only get one life, so you need to make the most of every moment.* And that's what I intend to do.'

I rolled my eyes. 'Whatever.'

He stood up. 'You won't be saying that when I become a pro basketball player, but I don't want you coming to any of my games because seeing your face will only irritate me.'

'And seeing your hideous face every day irritates me!' I barked, but Jesse just laughed as he lifted his rucksack off the back of the chair and swung it over his shoulder.

Mama dropped Jesse off first. His new secondary school, Sandall Rise, was huge, and as my brother got out of the car, I noticed that he looked quite nervous.

'I hope you're not saying goodbye without giving me

a kiss,' Mama called after him. Through the open window, she tapped her cheek, and as my brother turned round, his face was not only nervous but embarrassed.

'People are watching,' he whispered, his eyes glancing at the other kids making their way in.

'Don't be silly, Jesse. I'm your mother.'

Quickly, Jesse gave Mama a kiss then sprinted off with his head down and his rucksack slung over his shoulder.

A long time ago it used to be our dad who'd take us to school, but he left when I was six, blowing mine and Jesse's world apart. It's at times like this when I can't help but think about him. I'm sure if he'd still been in our lives, he would've been there taking photos, just like he did when I first started at Oak Nolan.

Mama dropped me off next but joined me inside, and as we waited for the school secretary to show me to my classroom, I suddenly realised something.

'I didn't pack my sketchbook!' I blurted out, feeling annoyed with myself, but Mama simply smiled.

'I'm sure you'll be far too busy making lots of new friends to have time to draw any pictures,' she said.

'Hello, I'm Mrs Sharma. Nice to meet you, Prune,' said the school secretary, coming out of her office. She shook both mine and Mama's hands. 'Your classroom is just down the corridor – 6D.'

Before Mama left I gave her a big hug and a kiss. And unlike Jesse, I didn't care who saw.

'Have a brilliant day, Prune,' she said, waving goodbye, but as soon as I walked down to my classroom, my heart began to race as all my worries returned like a tide come to sweep me away.

What if I don't fit in and make no friends at all?

'I think it's time to go in,' said Mrs Sharma as we stood outside the classroom.

I felt terrified and it was as if that terror had taken over my entire body, making me completely freeze as though my feet had been glued to the floor. Then, as Mrs Sharma opened the door, something quite unexpected happened. Wisps of clouds began to bloom around me, growing bigger and bigger until they were almost all I could see.

The colours were back.

CHAPTER 6

I felt pretty sure I was the only one who could see the clouds because no one else reacted, even as the colours flooded the entire classroom, their brightness making everyone dazzle like they were covered in glitter. And just as before, there were so many different shades of blue, red, green, purple, orange, yellow and every other hue imaginable. In fact, the number of colours seemed to be endless.

'Everyone, this is Prune,' said my new teacher, Mrs Downing, introducing me to the class.

Although I could hear her voice, I wasn't listening, my eyes gazing all around and even behind me. And the very fact I was seeing the colours here, I decided, meant my house couldn't be the source of the magic – if *magic* was indeed what the colours were.

Could the colours be coming from me? I wondered.

'What is she doing?' I heard someone say, and I promptly snapped out of it, focusing on Mrs Downing instead.

'Prune's new to the area. I hope you will all make her feel very welcome.'

She then indicated a table for me to sit at.

'Maybe she's one of those homeschooled kids who's never seen a classroom before,' said a girl with her hair in puffs.

As I walked past her table, she and the girl sitting next to her started giggling.

'Violet Thurman! Care to let me and the class know what you're finding so funny?' said Mrs Downing, frowning at the girl who'd made the comment.

'Nothing,' Violet mumbled.

'Well, be quiet then. The same goes for you, Melody,' said Mrs Downing to the other girl.

My seat was next to a boy with wavy brown hair wearing blue-rimmed glasses and a jumper that looked two sizes too big for him. He had the name Doug Spencer written on his exercise book. As I sat down he wiggled his eyebrows at me, which I figured was his way of saying hi.

But no sooner had I sat down than Mrs Downing had me standing straight up again to tell the class three things about myself. Feeling nervous, I took a few seconds to think of something before telling them that I'd moved to Delmere from Ocean View and was living in a house that had belonged to my grandparents. I thought that would count as two things, but Mrs Downing said it was only one. So I decided to tell them that I loved chocolate ice cream and that I had an older brother who annoyed me like crazy, and a couple of kids laughed because perhaps they could relate.

I felt a little more relaxed after that and started to think that maybe my new school might not be so bad, but that tiny bit of hope only lasted a short time because for the rest of the morning no one spoke to me. I couldn't help wishing I was back at my old school with my old friends. I spent all of breaktime wondering what Corinne was doing – handstands against a wall perhaps or playing hopscotch. Or maybe she was having a conversation with someone about a film she'd watched or a funny video she'd seen on YouTube. The thought of Corinne doing these things without me only left me feeling more glum. I wondered if she was sharing her KitKat bars with someone else like she'd shared them with me. I only hoped she wasn't calling that someone else her *new best friend*. I wondered too how Jesse was finding his new school – if he was feeling as lonely as I was.

*   *   *

Maple Lane really did feel different from Oak Nolan. For a start, it was much bigger and noisier, and at Oak Nolan there hadn't been colour clouds following me everywhere I went. It was like they'd replaced my shadow. As much as they were pretty, by lunchtime, the colour clouds had begun to get on my nerves, especially when I spotted Violet, Melody and another girl called Kirsten laughing at me. I'd been gazing at the colours, but I guess all they could see was me staring into thin air, which I imagined looked a bit odd. I just couldn't figure out why I was seeing the colours or where they were coming from.

Maybe there really is *something wrong with my eyes!* I thought.

Luckily the colours disappeared during my final lesson of the day – art. Mrs Downing asked us all to draw a picture of some pink lilies in a vase. And like I always do when I'm drawing, I went to that place in my head that fills me with happiness. Not only did I feel less daunted by my new school, but I also chatted with a girl called Amber, whose hair was in braids like mine and who had dimples pop up in her cheeks every time she smiled.

'This school may seem a bit scary,' she whispered as if she could read my mind, 'but it really isn't that bad. I've got a brother too who can be quite annoying, but he's much younger than yours. He's five and he's called Micah.'

'Well, I suppose Jesse's OK most of the time,' I said. 'I mean, he has always been there for me.'

That was true. Jesse might be a walking fart machine (he likes to call his farts *the silent assassins* because they smell so bad, you literally feel like you're dying), but he always knows how to cheer me up whenever I feel down, which is usually by making me his strawberry milkshake or making me laugh. Mama has banned us from eating biscuits after dinner, but if I've had a bad day, Jesse will sneak some up to my room, which we'll eat just before bed. When our dad left, we must have eaten more chocolate chip cookies than the Cookie Monster. Plus it was Jesse who stayed right by my side at Grandma Jean's funeral, my head leaning on his arm the whole time we were sat in the church as we listened to the eulogy and Grandma's favourite hymns, the choir's voices soaring higher than the church spire.

'I wish I could say the same for my brother,' said Amber, 'but I guess it's me who looks out for him, like making sure he doesn't make a mess with his Lego.'

It turned out Amber loved art just as much as I did and, like me, her favourite singer was Keirra Grace. Amber was really nice to me that day and even said that she liked the butterfly clips in my hair. I was very happy and relieved to make a new friend.

*　*　*

At the end of the lesson, Mrs Downing was very impressed with my picture. She told me that it looked very lifelike and that I had a talent for art, which of course I already knew. But it made me smile anyway. She even showed my picture to the rest of the class and told everyone how fantastic it was, which made my smile grow as wide as the lilies. Amber whispered, 'Well done!' And I felt really proud of myself. But from the corner of my eye, I could see Violet making a face.

Then she glanced in my direction and mouthed the word, '*Loser.*'

CHAPTER 7

When Mama got home from work she had with her a chicken and mushroom pizza from Big Sal's, which smelt delicious.

'I thought I'd treat you both to a pizza to celebrate your first day at your new schools,' she announced to me and Jesse. 'So tell me, how was it?' she asked me first as we laid the table and sat down to eat.

I wasn't sure what to say to Mama because her eyes looked so hopeful. Even though I'd enjoyed my art lesson, I couldn't stop thinking about Violet calling me a loser.

'It was great,' I lied, forcing a smile, but only because I wanted Mama to feel our move to Delmere was the fresh start she'd wanted it to be.

'And did you make any friends?'

'Yeah, a girl called Amber, who's very nice,' I answered truthfully.

I wanted to tell Mama about the colours I'd seen at school, but before I could she replied, 'That's wonderful,' and turned to Jesse. 'So how was your day?'

'It was all right,' he replied succinctly.

'Just all right?' said Mama, arching an eyebrow.

'Yeah.'

'And what are your teachers like?'

He shrugged. 'They're OK.'

'And does your school have a basketball team?' Mama asked.

'Yeah, but they have all the players they need. I put my name down on their waiting list though.'

'Well, let's hope your name won't be on that list for long and you'll get to join the team,' said Mama, smiling. 'Now, how about we tuck into this pizza?'

My chance to tell Mama about the colours finally came after dinner, when Jesse had gone up to his room, and Mama and I had moved on to the sofa to relax and digest our pizza.

'Mama, you know those colours I sort of mentioned to you before? I saw them again today, but no one can see them except me, which makes me think there could be something wrong with my eyes,' I told her all in a rush.

'And can you describe these colours?' she asked, her face looking concerned.

'It's sort of hard to describe because there's just so many, but they kind of look like clouds.'

It was clear from Mama's face, she didn't understand.

'I'll show you what they look like,' I said, getting up from the sofa.

I quickly ran upstairs and grabbed my sketchbook and pencils, and when I came back down I started to draw, but I couldn't do all the different shades of the colours because my pencil set only had one type of blue, pink, orange, yellow, green, purple, red and brown.

'This is what they look like, Mama, but there are even more colours,' I said, showing her my picture. 'Do you think I need to see an optician?'

'Well, I do think it would be worthwhile going for an eye test just to make sure everything's OK,' said Mama slowly.

'So do you think I might need glasses then?'

'You might, and if you do, then I'll make sure to get you a really nice pair,' said Mama, putting her arm around me. 'I'll book you an appointment with an optician, but in the meantime, I don't want you to worry about your eyes, OK?'

I nodded. 'OK.' I felt a little relieved because at least now I'd finally get to find out why I was seeing the colours.

'I'm sorry, but this seat's taken,' said Violet, when I went to sit next to her at lunch on Tuesday. She put her carton of juice on the chair to stop me from sitting down.

'Prune is such a funny name,' said Kirsten, who was sat opposite, and my cheeks felt hot with embarrassment.

'Don't be so mean, Kirsten,' said Melody, who was sitting beside her, but her face was just as sly, the three of them all staring at me as if I had measles.

It was obvious they didn't like me, but I wasn't going to let it bother me as I went and sat next to Doug at the very end of the table.

'If I were you, I wouldn't try to be their friend,' he whispered.

'Are they always that rude?' I whispered back.

'Yep.'

'Tell her about your special name for them,' said a boy from our class called Theo, who was sitting opposite.

I looked at Doug, who grinned.

'I call them the Vile-lets,' he said, which made me giggle, and I thought it served them right having a nickname like that, considering the way they'd just behaved was truly vile.

'Hardly any of us like them – well, none of the boys anyway,' said Theo.

'Violet is sort of their leader, while the other two just do what she tells them to,' said Doug. 'They hate me, but I hate them back just as much.'

'I don't think I like them either,' I said. 'But I don't know why they're being so nasty when I haven't done anything to them.'

'They just don't like anyone new,' Doug replied. 'I joined this school at the beginning of last term, and straight away they had it in for me, but I just try to ignore them and so should you,' he added as my rucksack, which I'd hung on the back of my chair, fell to the floor and my sketchbook slid out.

'What's that?' Doug asked.

'Oh, it's just my sketchbook,' I said, picking both it and my rucksack up.

'Can I take a look?'

'OK,' I said, passing it to him. 'I've only got a few pictures in there at the moment. It's pretty new.'

I had five pictures in total: a drawing of a model in a green dress, which I'd copied from a photo in one of Mama's magazines; a picture of a man standing in the rain, his face looking as bleak as the weather; and a picture of a patchwork quilt that had belonged to Grandma. She used to cover herself with it all the time when she'd sit in her armchair. Mama was now using the quilt to keep her warm at night, but she also told me it made her feel close to Grandma. Another picture was of a rainbow with a pot of gold at the end of it. When I was little I used to really believe there was gold at the end of a rainbow and once got Jesse to help me find it. But we didn't find any gold or the end of the rainbow. Instead, we found fifty pence and an old TV. We took the money and left the television. The fifth and final picture was my drawing of Groot.

'These are brilliant, Prune,' said Doug, flicking through. 'Especially the one of Groot. I love *Guardians of the Galaxy* – in fact I love every superhero film there is.'

'Me too,' I replied.

'And I love to watch all the TV shows,' said Doug.

'So who are your favourite superheroes?' I asked.

'Doctor Strange, followed by Aquaman, then Rocket from *Guardians*.'

'I like them as well, but my favourite superheroes are Captain Marvel, Black Panther and Superman.'

'So is drawing a hobby of yours?' asked Doug.

I nodded. 'But it's also what I want to do when I grow up. I'd love to have my pictures displayed in galleries all over the world.'

'Cool. I'm hoping to become a pilot. Did you know that the Airbus A319 is thirty-four metres in length?' said

Doug, adjusting his glasses – which were trying to escape down his nose – with a finger.

'No, I didn't know that.'

'I know loads of other facts about planes if you'd like to hear them.'

'Doug, I don't think she does,' said Theo, 'because, knowing you, we'll be here forever.'

'I don't mind,' I said politely.

Doug then proceeded to tell me everything he knew as I tried to look interested. But it all got a bit too technical for me to follow.

'But if I don't get to become a pilot, then I'd like to be an explorer. That way I'll still get to travel the world,' he finished.

'Hey, do you mind if I ask you something?' I said. 'When did you realise that you needed glasses?'

'Um, I can't remember because I've always been short-sighted,' said Doug. 'Do you have trouble seeing things that are far away?'

'No, but my eyes have been a bit funny recently,' I said.

'How do you mean?'

'My vision is sometimes a bit fuzzy,' I quickly replied.

While Doug seemed like a nice person, I didn't feel like telling him about the colours in case he thought I was making it up or was being silly.

'Well, if I could, I'd let you borrow my glasses, but I expect they'd be too strong for your eyes. But you can always have some of my carrots,' he offered. 'I don't actually like carrots that much, but they do say they're good for your eyes.'

I smiled as Doug kindly scraped his carrots on to my plate.

But as much as I *loved* carrots, I wasn't sure they'd do anything to solve whatever was wrong with my eyes.

CHAPTER 8

When I arrived home after school there was a letter on the mat addressed to Grandma Jean. I picked it up and opened it. The letter was from Grandma's dentist reminding her to book an appointment. I guessed Mama hadn't let them know that she'd died. Just thinking of Grandma again made me feel sad, and out of nowhere the colours began to appear – glorious greens, radiant reds, marvellous mauves, blissful blues and lots, lots more.

With my arms spread out, I twirled around, and the colours twirled too.

Is it me *making them move?*

I paused then shuffled my feet from side to side then rolled my arms and swung my hips, making up a dance routine, and it was as if the colours were dancing with me! I began to feel less sad and that's when the colours started to fade. It was like the colours were responding to me, depending on what I did and how I was feeling.

Are the colours linked to my emotions somehow? I wondered.

'What are you doing?' Jesse's voice rang out.

I'd been so caught up in my dancing that I hadn't heard him walk in.

'I'm dancing – what does it look like?' I said.

'Yeah, but who dances without music?' he replied with a scrunched face. 'It'd be like me playing basketball without a ball or like someone trying to tie their shoelaces with their teeth – as in nobody *normal* does that.'

'Haha, very funny,' I retorted.

Jesse went over to the fridge and took out a can of Pepsi, a tub of margarine and some ham. He then took some bread out of the cupboard and began to make a sandwich.

'Jesse, you know those colours I was telling you about?' I started to say. 'Well, I think how I'm feeling has got something to do with why they keep appearing.'

'Huh?' said Jesse, looking at me confused.

'It's been happening when I've been feeling sad, and they appeared at my school yesterday and I think it was because I was feeling scared with it being my first day.'

'I still don't quite get what you're on about, but I did learn that emotions come from a part of the brain called the limbic system, and the eyes of course are connected to the brain,' said Jesse, cutting his sandwich in two. 'So maybe there's something wrong with your brain, just like I always thought there was,' he jibed.

'Don't say that!'

'Look, sis, you've probably just scratched your cornea without realising and maybe that's what's causing you to see whatever these colours are. But apparently, the eyes are pretty resilient, so if it is a scratch, then it should heal up by itself.'

'How do you even know this stuff when you're always going on about how dull school is?'

'Well, I do pay attention sometimes, and I actually find science interesting.'

'But last night you didn't sound that thrilled about your new school.'

'You're right – I'm not thrilled,' said Jesse bluntly. 'But it's not as if I was going to like any school Mama sent me to. You might like it though when you start there in September.'

'Surely your school can't be that bad?'

'Says the girl who clearly loves her perfect new school, and by the sounds of it is already on her way to becoming the teacher's pet,' Jesse mocked.

'Um, I'm not sure that I do like my new school,' I admitted quietly. 'It's not as fun as Oak Nolan.'

'Looks like you could do with some cheering up. How about we go to Fern Park for a bit? We can sit in the sun and not think about school or anything else. And you can even show me some of your dance moves if you want, but I'll bring my iPod so you at least have some actual music to dance to.'

'Sounds good.' I smiled. 'But I'll only show you my moves if you promise to dance as well.'

'Ugh, how grim,' Jesse teased. 'But all right, I'll do it, so long as those dance moves don't involve me having to flap my arms like a chicken or jump up and down like a kangaroo.' He picked up his sandwich. 'Here, you can have this,' he said and offered me the other half.

'Thanks,' I replied as I took the sandwich and cheekily swiped his Pepsi as well.

CHAPTER 9

The next morning at school, I arrived at my class to find that we had a supply teacher as Mrs Downing was off sick. His name was Mr Novak, and when he started taking the register, he said everyone's names really loudly, and when he called out my name, and I replied, 'Here, Sir,' he said, 'I've not heard that name before. I've never really liked prunes,' which made the Vile-lets burst out laughing.

'Actual prunes, I mean. They tend to play havoc with my stomach,' Mr Novak quickly clarified, but I was left feeling so embarrassed.

And my day didn't get much better from there. At morning break I was walking across the playground to speak to Amber when Violet, who'd clearly noticed this, immediately scurried over to her. I was still a bit too far away to hear what Violet was saying, but I knew it was about me because Amber was looking in my direction. So I waited until Violet had walked off before I approached her.

'How's it going, Amber?' I said, trying to make my voice sound cheery, but inside I was anxiously wondering what Violet might have said to her.

'I'm OK, thanks,' Amber replied, but her voice was guarded.

'What do you think Mr Novak will ask us to draw in our art lesson?' I continued awkwardly.

Amber shrugged.

I shifted my feet. 'So what do you think of Keirra Grace's new song? Have you heard it yet?'

'Yeah, I like it,' said Amber quickly. 'I wish I could talk, Prune, but there's a book I want to take out of the school library, so I'll see you later.'

And before I had a chance to say anything else, Amber was running off and it was like she couldn't wait to get away from me fast enough. When I looked across the playground at the Vile-lets, they were all laughing hysterically, which made me feel furious. Like magic, my colour clouds began to appear and they seemed to blaze with an anger that matched my feelings.

I made my way over to Doug, who was leaning

against the wall, reading a magazine and like everyone else oblivious to the field of colours that was now covering the whole playground.

'I think Violet is trying to turn Amber against me,' I told him.

Of course, Doug did not seem surprised.

'Well, when I started here,' he said, 'she went around telling everyone I was weird and how they should stay away from me. And because of her, some kids still do.'

'But she shouldn't be able to get away with doing that.'

'I know, but it's not always easy to stand up to bullies,' said Doug quietly. 'You just have to hope they eventually get bored and leave you alone.'

I let out a long sigh as I tried to calm myself down, though I still felt quite angry.

'So what are you reading?' I asked Doug.

'It's one of my dad's magazines. It's all about aviation,' he replied and explained how it was his dad who'd inspired both his love of planes in general and his love of spotting planes, which was something they did regularly together.

This time I found myself listening with interest. I realised that in some ways Doug and I were very similar. We were both passionate about our hobbies and it turned out that we both share the same birthday, 23rd January. He was midway through telling me about his dad's friend who'd bought a small plane when Kirsten came strutting up, and I knew it wasn't a friendly chat she was looking for.

'Seriously, Doug, you are the weirdest person I have ever met,' she said, and the cheer in Doug's face instantly melted. 'I can see why you're friends with Prune because she's just as weird.'

I could tell Doug was hurt, but I tried to not let Kirsten's nasty comment upset me and looked at her with my arms folded as though I didn't care.

'Bullies like her always think they're the coolest,' said Doug once Kirsten had strutted off. 'If I had a power like Doctor Strange, I'd trap all bullies in another dimension so no one would ever have to fear them. And I'd start with the Vile-lets.'

'Hey, you know how some people change their names when they become famous or *infamous*?' I said to him.

Doug nodded.

'Well, I think they should change their names,' I said and pointed at each of them, 'to Vile-let Number One, Vile-let Number Two and Vile-let Number Three.'

I was glad to see another smile start to form on Doug's lips, but as the Vile-lets glared back at me, it was clear from their faces they weren't going to get bored of being horrible to me just yet.

CHAPTER 10

I was determined to not let the Vile-lets get me down and I tried to enjoy the rest of the day, but it seemed they had other ideas. When I went to the girls toilets during afternoon break, they followed me in, and this time I felt really nervous because there was no one else around and they were blocking the exit. My only choice was to rush into a cubicle and shut the door.

'Please just leave me alone,' I said as a multitude of colours gathered around me.

'Why should we leave you alone?! It's *you* who turned up at *our* school,' Violet taunted from the other side of the door. 'You're the one bothering us with your massive forehead.'

'Which is why from now on we're going to call you

Alienhead – because you look like a freakish alien,' said Kirsten as tears began to fill my eyes.

I've always been self-conscious of my high forehead ever since a boy called William Bailey used to tease me about it way back in Reception. He used to call me Bulkyhead, and there were many times I'd go home in tears. Though Mama would always give me a big cuddle and tell me how a high forehead was a sign of intelligence – and of beauty, because lots of top models had high foreheads. She'd even show me her copies of *Vogue* to prove her point.

'By the way, where did you get your rucksack?' said Violet now, making her voice sound friendly.

But I knew she was just being fake so I didn't respond.

'I only ask because it looks like something that you'd find on a rubbish dump. It's *so* disgusting.'

'Just like those butterfly clips she wears,' said Melody. 'They look like moths.'

'You got us told off by Mrs Downing the other day, and now you have that stupid Doug laughing at us. You really need to be taught a lesson,' said Kirsten.

'And you need to understand that at this school, *we're* in charge,' said Violet. 'You're so pathetic, Prune, always showing off like you're the star pupil.'

'I've not been showing off!' I replied as one of

them, presumably Violet, banged on the door to frighten me.

'*Do you like my picture, Mrs Downing?*' Violet mimicked, which made Melody and Kirsten howl with laughter as if it was the funniest impression they'd ever heard. 'Look, the only reason why Mrs Downing said it was fantastic is because you're new and she was trying to be kind, but we all know that picture was terrible. It looked more like vomit than lilies!'

'Too right, in fact that picture made me *want to* vomit,' said Melody. 'Plus it's your fault that Mrs Downing's off sick,' she added.

'What?' I murmured bewilderedly.

'She got sick at having to look at your big fat forehead,' Kirsten sneered.

'And don't expect Amber to be your friend, because I've told her all about you – how you're always staring into space like a right bozo. I also told her how you're someone who can't be trusted as you've been going around saying horrible things about Kirsten.'

'No I haven't!' I exclaimed, but all three of them just laughed.

They left the toilets, cackling loudly, and as I heard the door close behind them, I could no longer hold in my tears. They streamed down my face and fell through my colour clouds like shimmery raindrops.

* * *

I'm not sure how I got through the rest of the day. I just tried to keep my head down, and when the bell eventually sounded for the end of school, I just focused on getting home as quickly as possible. I found myself wishing more than anything that I could go back to my old school where people already knew and liked me, so when I got a call from Corinne that night, I can't tell you how happy it made me feel.

'School just isn't the same without you, Prune. I wish you were still here,' she said.

'I wish so too. My new school just isn't as good,' I replied, thinking about the Vile-lets. But I decided not to tell Corinne about them. I did tell her about Doug though and how nice he was. Then I said, 'Since we moved to Delmere I've been seeing these strange colours that no one else can see.'

'Whoa, that does sound strange. What's your mum said?'

'She's taking me to the optician to get an eye test. I'm hoping it won't be anything serious and might just mean I need glasses.' This was true. 'So, how have you been?'

'I joined the drama club, which has been fun. Miss Quinn says she could see me becoming a theatre star when I'm older, she thinks I'm that good.'

'That's nice,' I said, but I couldn't help feeling a little jealous that Corinne was doing something new and exciting without me.

'And how's everything else been? Is Mrs Hart still grumpy?'

'Yep, and today she got really angry with Lucas Miller. He got sent to Mrs Kingsbury's office, but it was his own fault. He kept trying to talk to Jacob when Mrs Hart was taking the register,' said Corinne. 'So, how are you finding it living in your grandma's old house?'

'It's been pretty good so far and it's *so* great not having to share a room with Jesse. But it has felt strange being here without Grandma Jean, and Delmere is definitely different from Ocean View.'

There aren't any tower blocks here in Delmere, so there are no kids living way up on the twelfth floor like Jesse and I used to in Ocean View. The whole town also feels much quieter with fewer shops than there were in our old town, and there's no basketball court in the local park, which is probably a big reason why Jesse thinks Delmere is completely dull. But I like the town, even though it could do with having a cupcake shop like the one we had on our old high street.

'Y'know, we should have another sleepover,' said Corinne, 'not this Saturday but the next.'

'Yeah, that'd be great,' I agreed.

Corinne and I always have the best sleepovers. We sit up listening to Keirra Grace songs or watch our favourite films.

We decided that we'd have our next sleepover at my place, seeing as Corinne hadn't seen our house yet. I could hear Corinne's mum calling her in the background telling her that her dinner was ready.

'I've got to go, Prune, but I hope your eye test goes OK.'

'I am still your best friend, aren't I, and no one else?' I quickly blurted.

'Course, and you always will be, forever,' said Corinne.

But as I put down the phone, for a moment I found myself doubting that Corinne would want to stay best friends with me. I mean, who would want to be friends with a bozo who sees colours that she can't be sure are even there? Deep down though, I knew the doubt I was feeling was because I'd let the Vile-lets get to me. *Of course* Corinne would always be my best friend.

I really hoped getting my eyes sorted would mean the Vile-lets would stop making fun of me. My appointment with the optician really couldn't come soon enough.

CHAPTER 11

'So are you looking forward to your appointment with the optician next week?' said Jesse as we walked to school on Thursday.

I shrugged.

'I did think you'd be a bit more excited, because you never know, they might just discover you have a special colour-seeing superpower,' Jesse quipped. 'I've got a joke for you. What did the chicken say to the duck with a superpower?'

'I dunno – what did it say?'

'Why, duck, your powers are quack-tacular!' said Jesse, and we both giggled.

'Actually, I wouldn't mind if they do discover I have a superpower, because I'd be able to become a superhero and zap you out of existence.'

'Oh, really now!' Jesse laughed. 'So come on – what would you call yourself if you were a superhero?'

'Um … I think I'd call myself Prune the Amazing.'

'Amazing, huh? You sure it wouldn't be Prune the Terribly Annoying?'

I poked him in the ribs.

'OK, OK – you can call yourself Prune the Most Wonderful. Or how about, Prune the Magnificent?'

'Much better,' I agreed.

'Seriously though, I hope they get to the bottom of what's making you see those colours,' said Jesse, as we reached his school.

I was about to reply when a car pulled up on the other side of the road. Two boys jumped out and a much taller boy stepped out of the driver's seat who I instantly recognised as Bryce. And the very sight of them made me shudder.

Ugh. What do they want? I thought.

And as if on cue, my colour clouds appeared, the landscape transforming around us. And I found myself noticing hues that I hadn't noticed before – crimson, khaki, peach, jade, maroon, burgundy, sapphire and aquamarine.

'What are you guys doing here?' said Jesse, looking surprised to see them as they strolled over.

'We're on our way to see my cousin Connor,' said

Bryce. 'I'm sure I told you that he lives in Delmere. Anyway, I thought as we're in the neighbourhood, we'd come and see how you were doing.'

'I'm good, thanks,' said Jesse.

As the colours swirled around me, I wished I was brave enough to tell the boys to get lost.

'So, you got any plans today?' said one of the boys.

'Well, as you can see, Nathan, I'm just about to head into school,' said Jesse.

'But going in there isn't going to be as exciting as hanging out with us. So why not just forget about school for today?' said Bryce, and my heart began to thump.

'No, Jesse, you can't!' I blurted out. 'Don't you remember the promise you made to Mama not to skip school? Please don't go with them.'

The boys surveyed me, their horrible, toad-like eyes feeling like lasers shooting into my skull. I quickly turned away from their glare. Why couldn't the colours have been like a river and washed them away?

'So you take orders from your sister do you?' said the other boy.

'No, Zack! I don't!' said Jesse and stared at me angrily. 'I'm my own boss. I decide what I do.'

'Once we've seen my cousin, then we can all go back to Ocean View and do some training at my gym,' said Bryce.

'That sounds great,' my brother replied, 'but I think

I'll have to give it a miss what with it being my first week at this school.'

'You're not letting me down are you, Jesse? Because that's something I *really* hate people doing,' said Bryce, his voice becoming agitated. 'Plus, I'd hate for there to be any problems.'

He gave my brother a hard stare as he cracked his knuckles. I gulped and so did Jesse. My brother had already told me what Bryce does when people get on the wrong side of him, and it nearly always involved his fists.

'I mean, you don't see me letting people down,' said Bryce. 'Did I let you down that time when I battered that kid who was bullying you?' He smiled, but it was a smile that was more threatening than friendly.

'N-n-n-o, Bryce – I'm not l-l-letting you down,' Jesse stammered. 'And I'll, um … always be grateful for what you did back then.'

'So does that mean you'll come and hang out with us?' said Bryce.

'Yeah, course I will,' Jesse replied quickly.

'Excellent. Y'know for a minute there, I thought you'd gone all nerdy on us and was beginning to wonder if this boring school might already be rubbing off on you.'

'Nah, there's no chance of that. I can't stand the place,' said Jesse.

'Well, we best get going then,' said Bryce and headed back towards the car.

But as Jesse went to go with him and the others, I grabbed his arm.

'Don't, Jesse, please. I know you don't really want to go with them.'

He shook his arm free.

'Stop embarrassing me, Prune!' he squawked.

'Are you coming or what?' said Nathan, as he, Zack and Bryce got back into the car.

'Yeah, just a minute,' my brother called out.

'Are you seriously willing to miss school for those morons?' I asked.

'Don't call my friends that!'

'We moved here because Mama wanted things to be better for us, but it's like you just want to mess everything up. You're so selfish, Jesse, d'you know that?'

'I'm not messing anything up. And if anyone's selfish then it's Mama, because she was the one who wanted us to move to this stupid town, not me.'

'I'm worried, Jesse. I'm worried you're going to get kicked out of school just like Bryce.'

'I won't get kicked out. I'm only missing a day,' he said, like bunking off school was no worse than blowing your nose without a tissue.

'But what if you *do* get kicked out? Mama will be so upset.'

'Oh, just go away, Prune!' he said then pushed me hard, making me almost fall over.

I could hear the boys laughing, but what made it worse was that Jesse was laughing with them. But I'd come to learn that Jesse was always a different person whenever Bryce was around. And he'd been like that ever since they became friends, which was around the same time Poppa B died. That's when Jesse began to misbehave a lot. He was always coming back late from the park and kept being cheeky to Mama, plus every word out of his mouth was *Bryce this* and *Bryce that*.

'That's what you get for trying to tell me what to do,' my brother jeered then strode off to the car.

As I walked on towards my school, hot tears filled my eyes. Of course I knew deep down Jesse didn't mean to be cruel – it was the idiots he called friends who made him act like that. And for all I knew, what they were really planning to do was to go shoplifting, which caused a thought to suddenly gnaw at me.

What if Jesse gets into even bigger trouble this time?

Not only would that crush Mama's heart but mine too.

If only there was a way I could stop Jesse from ruining his life, I thought.

The problem was I had no idea how to help him.

CHAPTER 12

It was finally Monday, the day of my appointment at the optician, and I couldn't wait to finish my cornflakes so that Mama and I could get going. All weekend, I'd been thinking about it as well as other stuff, mostly the Vilelets. Well, thinking of ways I could avoid them even though that seemed to be virtually impossible.

When I'd eventually arrived at school on Thursday after watching Jesse drive off to goodness knows where with Bryce and his minions, all three girls were stood waiting at the gate, and as soon as I walked in they followed me, saying 'Alienhead' over and over. Of course they made sure no teachers were nearby when they did it. Then, they did the same thing on Friday, as well as giving me evils all day. There was nowhere I could go or even look without them getting at me.

I'd also spent the weekend thinking about Jesse, worrying what things Bryce might be trying to get him to do, and that worry kept making the colour clouds appear and loom over me like a giant.

'I hope you've been giving your homework as much attention as you've been giving that phone,' said Mama to Jesse at breakfast. 'And just who precisely are you texting?' she asked irately.

'Just a boy in my class,' he said. 'And if you must know, it's actually about a history task we have to do. I've been asking him questions about it.'

Mama's face immediately softened, whereas I looked at Jesse with suspicion. I had a feeling it was really Bryce he was sending texts to, which made me worry that he was planning to bunk off again.

I felt a lot less worried though later that morning, once Mama had dropped Jesse off at school and I'd watched him walk through the gates.

During my appointment the optometrist, who was called Kofi, got me to read letters on a chart that started big then gradually got smaller until they were teeny tiny. But I was able to read them all. There was a test where I had to focus on an object while he separately covered each of my eyes with something that looked like a spoon. I also passed that test, along with one he gave me to check if I was colour blind. It was strange to have that particular test because I definitely knew that wasn't the problem. I couldn't stop seeing colours!

'Your eyes are absolutely fine, Prune, so you won't be needing glasses,' said Kofi.

'That's a relief,' said Mama. 'Although, if her eyes are fine, then why is Prune seeing these colour clouds she describes?'

'It could be caused by migraines. There is something called kaleidoscope vision where the brain causes your eyes to see flashes of colours or dots or lines,' said Kofi. 'Do you ever find that you get headaches, Prune?'

'No, not really. Unless you count my brother, Jesse – he's a real headache,' I said, which made him laugh.

But I only made that joke to bat away my worried feelings.

If it wasn't my eyes that were the problem, then could Jesse be right that there was something wrong with my brain? Just what was making the colours appear? Could there still be a chance it was magic?

I so badly wanted to figure it all out. I couldn't stand not knowing any longer.

'The optometrist did say the kaleidoscope vision is likely to be temporary,' said Mama as she drove me to school afterwards, 'so please don't fret, Prune.'

'But what if I end up needing an operation or something?' I replied.

'Well, that's why it's always good to get these things checked out, just like the optometrist said.'

'So you think there's something wrong with my brain too?'

'We won't know, Prune, until you've seen the doctor. But are you sure you haven't been suffering from migraines?'

I shook my head. 'Though the colours do only seem to appear when I'm feeling certain emotions, like if I'm feeling upset.'

'Do they? Why didn't you tell me this before? What's been making you upset?' said Mama, now looking more worried than I felt.

'I've just been missing Grandma,' I murmured, not mentioning the Vile-lets.

'Well, that's understandable,' said Mama. 'But Dr Connelly should be able to tell us more, so I'll book you an appointment.'

I arrived at school towards the end of lunch. My class had already finished eating and were in the playground, so I had to eat my lunch by myself. And just as I was about to tuck into my apple crumble dessert, a girl in my class called Willow came up to me.

'Hi, Prune. I've been asked to give you this,' she said, handing me a folded piece of paper.

I opened the note and read it:

You're not wanted, Alienhead.

I of course knew immediately who it was from.

I got up and sped off to the toilets, tears spilling down my face as the colour clouds started to blossom around me – steel blues, mustard yellows, flamingo pinks, coffee browns, lime greens, ruby reds and thousands more. I felt so upset and would've done anything to have been back at my old school with Corinne and my other friends. Sitting in a cubicle, I took out my sketchbook and began to draw a picture of a hot-air balloon. I coloured the balloon blue and yellow with a green zigzag at the bottom.

I stared at the picture as I imagined being in a balloon just like it, one that would take me far away from the Vile-lets and Maple Lane School.

'I don't want to be here!' I cried. 'Take me away from this school – please take me away,' I said over and over as I wished for the balloon to be real.

All of a sudden the colours started to move, spinning and spinning until they'd narrowed into a funnel right above my sketchbook. Feeling alarmed, I dropped the sketchbook and squeezed my eyes shut, hoping the colours would go away.

What's happening?!

After a few seconds, I could hear a commotion coming from outside and quickly reopened my eyes. The colours were gone and from the sound of it, everyone was excited for some reason.

Wiping my tears with my sleeve, I stuffed my sketchbook back into my rucksack and headed out. Kids and teachers were all running towards the exit. I hurried out as well but then froze when I saw what was causing the excitement, my mouth practically hitting the ground.

In the middle of the playground was a hot-air balloon.

Not only that, but the balloon was blue and yellow with a green zigzag. It was *identical* to the balloon I'd drawn!

Nobody could believe their eyes, least of all me.

How could this even be possible?

My heart started to thud.

'There's nobody in the basket,' said Mrs Mahoney, the deputy head, who was trying to keep everyone away from it. (All the kids secretly call her Moody Mahoney because she's the grumpiest teacher at Maple Lane.)

'So how did it get here?' said another teacher, called Miss Parsons.

In amongst the crowd, I spotted Doug and made my way over.

'Do you know where that came from?' I asked him.

'It just appeared out of nowhere, but it's so cool, don't you think?' said Doug.

'I guess so,' I muttered, feeling completely astonished.

'I wonder who it belongs to,' said a boy in our class called Oliver.

'Maybe someone famous,' said Doug.

Is it my *balloon?* I thought to myself, feeling slightly panicked. *No, it can't be – can it?*

I took out my sketchbook and flipped through the pages until I got to the picture of my hot-air balloon, but it was just a blank page.

I quietly gasped.

Where had my picture gone?

'Everyone inside, please. I'm sure there's a simple explanation for this,' said our head teacher, Mr Nelson, as he and other teachers started to usher us back inside.

For the rest of the day, the hot-air balloon was all anyone spoke about, but I was in too much shock to join in and I couldn't stop wondering if it was me who'd made the balloon appear. The colours had never turned into a funnel before, nor had any of my pictures just disappeared from my sketchbook. It was like the colours had somehow brought the hot-air balloon to life.

So was that it? Had the colours made my picture *real*? And if so, how?

I needed answers, and the only way I was going to get them was to draw another picture.

CHAPTER 13

As soon as I got home I whisked out my sketchbook and, sitting at the kitchen table, I began to draw a picture of a bowl of popcorn.

I knew the colours were connected to my feelings as they always appeared when I was feeling sad, worried, angry or scared, but was there a way I could make them *deliberately* appear?

I tried staring at the picture to see if that would do the trick, but nothing happened. I then jiggled my sketch-book, hoping that would make the colours appear, but again nothing happened. I let out a sigh of frustration. I sat at the table mulling over the events of my day in as much detail as possible, my mind retracing my steps to when I saw the hot-air balloon in the playground. And as

I thought about the horrible note the Vile-lets had written, I found myself feeling angry and upset again, and slowly my colour clouds began to emerge – lilac, cyan, bronze, fuchsia, apricot, indigo – all billowing and thickening around me.

So now that the colours were here, I just needed to figure out how to make them turn my picture into a real bowl of popcorn. I stared at the picture again, but it wasn't leaping out of the page. In fact, it wasn't doing anything at all.

What was it that I did differently to make the hot-air balloon appear?

I scratched my head in thought.

I remembered wishing to have a hot-air balloon come to carry me away and that I'd wanted that to happen so badly. More than I'd ever wanted anything.

Was that how I made it happen?

Even though I had drawn lots of other pictures since the colours first appeared, none of those had come to life. It had to be my *wishing* for the hot-air balloon to be real that had made it happen!

I looked at my picture again and began to wish.

'Please, please become a real bowl of popcorn,' I said in my mind, wishing as hard as I could.

Instantly, the colours responded. It was as if they could hear my thoughts as they began to spin faster and faster, forming a funnel. And I watched, totally stunned, as my picture rose from the page and was sucked straight into it. The colours swiftly vanished from the air and, just like magic, a bowl of popcorn appeared on the table. I looked back at my sketchbook. The picture had disappeared.

I did it! I made my picture come to life!

For a few minutes, I just gazed at the bowl, fully awestruck.

It really was incredible.

Very carefully I dipped my hand into the bowl and popped some of the popcorn into my mouth and chewed. It was real popcorn, plus it was warm, just how I like it.

I was truly amazed.

Could I bring other drawings to life? I looked through my sketchbook. Like my picture of Groot or my picture of a rainbow?

And what if I drew a pair of shoes or a couple of chihuahuas – would they become real?

Or what if I wanted to bring to life something really spectacular like a space rocket?! Would that work too?

My mind had more questions than a police detective.

And how was I even able to bring my pictures to life? Was it some sort of special power? A *superpower*?

Could other people in my family do it? Could

Grandma or Poppa B? He used to like drawing. Or did my dad have a superpower? Maybe that's why he left us – because he wanted to become a secret crime-fighting superhero.

I let that thought stay with me for a bit, even though deep down I knew it was unlikely that my dad was out there saving the world. But it certainly felt like a nicer thought than the one that continued to linger – that he'd left simply because he didn't love us any more.

I wondered what Mama and Jesse would make of my superpower. Would they think it was the best thing they'd ever seen? I expected Jesse would want me to bring something to life like a personal gym. Not that I'd mind doing it if it kept him away from Bryce.

As I continued pondering all the possibilities, Jesse arrived home.

'Jesse, I've got something to tell you!' I said immediately.

'Sorry, Prune, I've got no time to chat. I've got things to do,' he replied, heading straight to the kitchen cupboard and taking out a packet of crisps.

'But it's something amazing, Jesse.'

He turned round. 'Why can I smell popcorn?'

'That's what I'm trying to tell you! I drew—'

'You know you're not allowed to use the cooker without supervision,' he said, wandering over … And that's when I noticed his feet – or should I say, the expensive-looking trainers on his feet.

I gawped. 'Where did you get those from?'

'Bryce got them for me.'

'And where did *he* get them from?'

'He bought them online – not that it's got anything to do with you.'

'Why is he buying you trainers?'

'What's with the interrogation?' said Jesse, sucking his teeth.

'OK, if you don't want me asking you questions, then I'm sure Mama will be happy to ask them.'

'Yes – and I'm sure she'll want to know why you almost burned the house down making popcorn,' Jesse retorted.

'That's a lie! I didn't almost burn it down.'

'Yeah, yeah,' said Jesse sarcastically. 'But no need to panic – I won't say anything if you don't tell her about my trainers.'

I rolled my eyes but agreed to keep quiet. But as Jesse wandered out, I suddenly had a sinking feeling.

Had Bryce really bought Jesse those trainers or had he stolen them?

CHAPTER 14

I wanted to tell Mama about my special ability as soon as she got in, but thanks to Jesse I didn't get the chance. Before she'd even hung up her jacket she was shouting up to my brother from the bottom of the stairs. But he couldn't hear because he was playing his music really loudly. So she took off one of her shoes and started beating it against the staircase.

'Jesse Arnold Robinson! You get yourself down here right now!'

When my brother emerged a minute later, his face looked unfazed.

'So, just *when* were you going to tell me your school has excluded you for three days?! And you're lucky it's only that! I got a call from your head teacher letting me know how you skipped school last Thursday *and* today!'

Jesse said nothing while I looked at him aghast.

I couldn't believe he'd been excluded. It quickly dawned on me that when Mama and I dropped Jesse off on our way to the optician, he must've snuck off as soon as he'd thought the coast was clear. I had hoped the previous Thursday had been a one-off. But knowing Jesse had bunked off again made me feel like I couldn't trust him and even more sure it had been Bryce he'd been texting over breakfast.

'What I'd like to know is where you've been going,' said Mama, looking as furious as the Hulk when he's busting out of his clothes.

But Jesse remained shtum.

'Answer me, boy!' Mama boomed then sucked her teeth. 'I don't know why I'm even bothering to ask because I already know. You've been going back to Ocean View, haven't you? And no doubt you've been hanging around Bryce and those other hooligans.'

Jesse looked Mama straight in the eye. 'No.'

'Don't lie to me, Jesse!' Mama scowled. 'Why do you keep doing this? What is wrong with you? Don't you care about your education?' She directed her questions at the ceiling as if she was looking to find the answers written across the paintwork. She shook her head. 'You've only been at that school for five minutes. I was really hoping things would be different once we'd moved, but it seems not.'

'I hate that rotten school!' Jesse blurted. 'I'm not learning anything there that I don't already know. And none of it is stuff I'm going to need when I'm a pro basketball star. Plus, most of the kids are geeks.'

'Well, maybe you can learn something from those *geeks*, as you call them, because you're certainly not going to learn anything from those yobs back in Ocean View—'

'I wish we'd never moved to Delmere. Why couldn't you have just let me stay at my old school?'

'You mean the school you hardly turned up to? The school that was debating whether to kick you out? Is that the one you mean?' said Mama.

'At least I had some friends there.'

'Yeah, friends who were skipping school themselves,' Mama retorted.

'But I wasn't a loner like I am now,' Jesse replied, and I couldn't help but feel sorry for my brother. I'd had no idea he'd been struggling to make friends at his school. I definitely knew what that felt like.

'Then join a club or something – get to know people,' said Mama. 'But no more skipping school!' She crossed her arms and puffed out a breath. 'Right, once your exclusion is over, I'll be taking you to school every day and you're not going to miss a single lesson – do you hear me?'

Jesse stayed silent.

'Well, if you're not going to say anything, you're best off just getting out of my sight,' Mama grumbled.

'Fine by me,' said my brother, then skulked back up to his room.

'And I want you to stay away from Bryce!' Mama yelled after him. 'He might live in a posh house, but that boy is bad news!'

We heard Jesse's door slam then blaring music as he turned his stereo right up, the bass stomping like a bear across the ceiling. Mama beat her shoe against the staircase again.

'Turn that noise off! There'll be no loud music tonight – do you understand?!'

Jesse turned it down but not off. Mama sucked her teeth again and mumbled something under her breath. Then she put her shoe back on and went into the living room, slumping down on to the sofa. I went and sat in Grandma's old armchair and could see that Mama's eyes were shiny with tears.

'All I ever wanted was the best for you kids and for you to be happy. But it's like Jesse's desperate to ruin his future. He might think Bryce is going places, but I don't think that boy has done anything since they kicked him out of school.'

She exhaled a long breath.

'If only there was some other way I could get through to that boy,' she muttered as I noticed her eyes glance at a framed photograph on the mantelpiece.

It was a photo of my dad, and only one of a few that we still have of him, the rest tucked away in a black leather album with mine and Jesse's baby pictures.

I still don't know why my dad walked out; Mama's never explained the reason, but she's always said that we're better off without him. I'm not even sure where my dad is right now. Last we heard, through an old friend of his, was that he was living in Paris, working in a hotel. But that was four years ago.

'Prune, you don't wish we hadn't moved to Delmere, do you?' asked Mama now.

'No, I like it here.'

'And things are still going OK at school?'

I would've preferred to have told Mama the truth — that I didn't like my new school either — but as she was already upset, I didn't want to give her anything else to be concerned about. And the last thing I wanted was for her to think us moving to Delmere had been a complete disaster.

'Yeah, it's all good. I'm really enjoying it and every-one's so friendly,' I burbled, a little too enthusiastically, but I don't think Mama noticed.

'If only your brother could feel the same about his school, then maybe things would be better,' said Mama wearily.

Despite wanting to tell Mama how I'd brought my pictures to life, and maybe even show her, now just didn't feel like the right time. So instead I offered her a hug as I didn't like seeing her look so sad.

'You're a good girl, Prune,' she said, and I was pleased my hug managed to bring a smile to her face.

CHAPTER 15

When I woke up the next morning, I wondered if the previous day had all been a dream.

Had I really brought to life the hot-air balloon and popcorn?

I checked my sketchbook. The pages where I'd drawn both the hot-air balloon and the bowl of popcorn were still blank. So it wasn't a dream! I *did* have a superpower! It was still hard to believe. I mean, only superheroes like Captain Marvel or Gamora from *Guardians of the Galaxy* had those – not regular kids like me.

I did a huge jump for joy and at last I felt that I understood the colours. It was clear they had a purpose, which was to bring my pictures to life. I couldn't stop wondering what I could use my superpower for. Maybe I really could become a superhero. The possibilities were endless!

At school everyone was still talking about the hot-air balloon, with kids wanting to know where it had come from, who it belonged to, and why couldn't we keep it. If only they knew it was me who'd brought it to life. I'm not sure what they'd say, though I doubt it would stop the Vile-lets from being any less horrid to me. But Doug might be impressed.

There was a rumour going round that Mr Nelson had flown home in the balloon and was storing it in his garage. Even if that was true, I didn't exactly want the balloon back because it wasn't as if there was anywhere in our house to store it.

'I wonder if he'll use the balloon to go travelling in,' said Theo while I was chatting to him and Doug during morning break.

'Well, if I was Mr Nelson, the first country I'd visit would be Japan,' said Doug. 'For ages I've been asking my mum and dad if we can go there for our summer holiday, but the only place they ever want to go to is Ireland, where my grandparents live. Where would you go, Prune, if you were able to just fly away in a balloon?'

I almost told Doug I would've flown straight back to my old school, but instead I told him, 'I think I'd go to

Australia so I could see a koala up close. I think they're really cute.'

'I wish I had the power to teleport myself anywhere I wanted to go, like Doctor Strange – then I wouldn't even need a balloon or a plane. And I could still make sure I was home in time for dinner,' said Doug.

'Have you ever thought there might be real people in the world with superpowers?' I asked him as I wondered for the first time if there were other kids out there just like me.

'Yeah, I think there are,' Theo cut in before Doug could answer. 'I've seen them on YouTube. There's this one video of a woman in a supermarket who disappears then magically reappears in another aisle within seconds. It was obvious she had teleportation powers.'

'Those videos aren't real,' said Doug dismissively. 'They all use special effects to make you believe that there are people with superpowers. I've seen a couple of videos myself of people flying through the air, but you can so tell it's fake. Plus, I've seen a video where they've tried to make out a person is a time traveller because they're speaking into what looks like a mobile phone in an old black-and-white film. But I don't believe any of it.'

'Which I guess means you're not going to believe there are people in this town who have superpowers,' said Theo.

I gulped as Theo's eyes darted back and forth between me and Doug.

Had he guessed I have a superpower?

'What are you talking about?' asked Doug.

'I'm talking about Delmere being a magical place – well, that's what some people say, don't you know?' Theo began to whisper excitedly.

But Doug and I just looked at him completely mystified.

'My gran said when she was a kid there was a boy who lived next door to her who could fly, and she swears she saw him flying across the street when she was looking out of her window one night.'

'It was probably something she dreamed,' said Doug airily.

'No, she's certain she wasn't dreaming,' said Theo.

'And if the boy *did* have a superpower, did it just appear one day?' I asked, thinking of my own power.

Theo shrugged. 'I dunno, but I do know from my gran that when Delmere was just a little village thousands of years ago, there was a creature that lived under the earth that would rise every so often to feast on the souls of the children—'

'Rubbish!' scoffed Doug.

'No, go on – I want to hear this,' I pressed.

'Only one year the kids fought back,' said Theo. 'They'd somehow gained these different superpowers, which they unleashed on to the creature, destroying it once and for all. And legend has it that the energy from the kids' powers got absorbed into the ground, which years and years later became Delmere, the town it is today. And throughout the centuries some believed that energy caused other kids to develop superpowers just like the boy my gran knew. That's why they call it the Delmere Magic. So for all we know, there are kids right here in this school who have superpowers.'

I briefly lowered my eyes.

'And there was me thinking that the only exciting thing about this town was the ice-cream parlour off the high street,' said Doug. 'Still, I don't believe it.'

'Y'know I'm sure I've heard a similar story to what you've just told us,' I said to Theo, trying to wrack my brain as to where I might've heard it.

Could it have been in a book I read?

'That's because it most probably is a story that Theo's made up,' said Doug, shaking his head.

'I didn't make it up!' Theo insisted.

Still, it all made me wonder. If Theo was telling the truth, then there really were other kids with superpowers – kids who might even be living on my street.

'Didn't that hot-air balloon remind you of someone?' Violet's voice rang out abruptly as she and the other Vile-lets walked past.

'Yeah, it did. It reminded me of someone with an enormous forehead,' Kirsten replied.

Of course, I knew they were talking about me and were trying to get a reaction.

'Just ignore them,' muttered Doug.

I nodded, trying my best to do this.

'So are you planning on doing any plane spotting this week?' I asked.

But before Doug could respond, at the top of her voice, Violet boomed, 'I'm actually glad that balloon has gone. I only wish another fat-headed monstrosity would go too.'

And with that, I leaped up from the bench where we were sitting.

'I um … need to go to the toilet,' I said to Doug and Theo, doing all I could to keep my voice steady.

I even smiled, though I could feel it wobbling as the colours began to surround me. But I didn't want the Vile-lets or anyone else to see how upset I was as I fled the playground and ran to the toilets, tears springing from my eyes. Even with a superpower I felt so helpless, and again I just desperately wanted to escape.

I could bring to life a bike, I thought suddenly as I slammed the cubicle door shut behind me.

That way I could cycle as fast as I could out of this school. I sat down on the closed toilet and pulled my sketchbook out of my rucksack, but just as I was about to start my drawing, someone knocked on the door.

'Are you OK, Prune?'

It was Melody.

'Go away!' I yelled at her.

'What Violet and Kirsten said was really mean,' she uttered slowly. 'I told them they shouldn't have said it.' She paused for a minute. 'But do you know what Violet said to me?'

'I don't actually care,' I responded, drying my eyes.

'She said she didn't want to be my friend,' Melody prattled on anyway. 'And do you know what I said?'

I didn't answer.

'I said "suits me", because I'm sick and tired of being horrid like they are.' She went silent again and I heard her step closer to the door. 'Prune, I'm sorry for being mean to you. I was just going along with Violet … She was the one who made me call you names. Will you forgive me? Not that I'd blame you if you didn't.'

'So are you saying you're not friends with Violet any more?' I asked warily.

'Yeah. And to be honest, I don't even have any friends now. Violet and Kirsten were the only friends I had.'

I wasn't sure whether to believe what she was saying.

I came out of the cubicle and stood face to face with Melody, who looked sheepish.

'And how do I know you're telling the truth?' I challenged.

'You can ask Doug and Theo. They saw when Violet basically told me to get lost,' said Melody.

'Oh, I'm not interested,' I growled and went back into the cubicle.

'Sorry, Prune,' said Melody, and I waited until I could hear she'd left the toilets before I opened my sketchbook again.

But instead of drawing a bike, I started to draw a scarf, one that I wanted to be all snugly like Grandma's quilt. Once I was finished I began to wish quietly, over and over, for the scarf to come to life. Automatically, the colours started to twist into a funnel that sucked my picture up from the page. A brief second later a chunky scarf lay on my lap. I gently stroked it, feeling awestruck all over again that I could actually bring my drawings to life.

I wrapped the scarf around me and breathed in its warmth. After about a minute I noticed something. The scarf was getting longer. I took it off and threw it to the floor as right before my eyes the scarf began to grow and grow and grow! The scarf was ... out of control!

I tried to leave the cubicle, but I was trapped,

getting caught up in the scarf like an insect in a spider's web. I speedily tried to untangle myself and at the same time reach for the door. Only my left arm was stuck, and as I tried to pull it free, I seemed to just make things worse as I got even more tangled up. It was like I was in a huge wrestling match with the scarf – tugging, pushing and kicking it. After more untangling, I finally managed to free myself and reach for the lock on the cubicle door. I ran for the exit, and straight into Amber and Willow.

'You can't go in there!' I said to them, blocking their way.

'But I need the toilet,' said Willow, trying to get past.

'No, there's … there's something in there.'

There was no way I could let them see the scarf. What if it was still growing?

'Like what?' said Amber, which incidentally was the first time she'd spoken to me since that day in the playground.

'What's going on here?' Mrs Mahoney came striding over.

'Prune won't let us use the toilet,' said Willow.

'Oh, and why's that?' said Moody Mahoney, her eyes glaring suspiciously.

'Because … there's a big hairy spider,' I said, blurting out the first thing I could think of.

Amber automatically sprang back. 'Eek! I hate spiders!'

'Me too,' Willow echoed. 'It's OK – we'll use another toilet.'

And the two of them hastily scuttled off.

'Enough with the exaggeration, Prune. Now, will you please stand aside,' said Moody Mahoney, her nostrils flaring like a bull about to charge.

'You really don't want to see it, miss – trust me. The spider is as big as a football.'

But Moody Mahoney just looked at me like I was telling tales. Not that she'd be wrong.

'Are you hiding something in there?'

'No,' I said, shaking my head.

'Well, if you're not, then please step aside.'

I was desperate for the scarf not to be in there.

'Please be gone,' I said in my mind, over and over, desperately imagining it was no longer there.

'Come on now – shift,' said Moody Mahoney impatiently.

I slowly moved away from the door and held my breath as I followed her in.

'I can't see any spider,' she said, looking in each cubicle.

I took a peek into the cubicle where the scarf had been, only it wasn't there any more, and all my breath came out in a big sigh of relief.

So, I realised, to make something vanish, all I

needed to do was imagine it gone. My sketchbook, however, was still in the cubicle. In my hurry to get out, I'd left it behind. Moody Mahoney picked it up.

'I presume this is yours?' she said.

I nodded as she handed it to me.

'Are you sure you really did see a spider?' said Moody Mahoney, tilting her head.

I nodded again.

'Well, I expect it was a lot more afraid of you than you were of it.'

Moody Mahoney looked at her watch. 'Breaktime is nearly over, so you'd best hurry along. I wouldn't want you to be late back to class.'

She escorted me back out of the toilets.

Once she'd disappeared down the corridor, I looked in my sketchbook and my picture of the scarf was there again. I gasped, not because the picture was back on the page, but because the scarf wasn't how I'd drawn it. Instead of stretching around the page, it was just on one side and looked all crumpled. It was clear there was more to my superpower than I'd thought, but one thing was for sure – I urgently needed to get a handle on it before it got out of control again.

CHAPTER 16

In the playground at lunchtime I was hanging out with Theo and Doug when Melody came over. She wanted them to convince me that it was true she'd fallen out with Violet. Not that I cared much.

'They can tell you Violet said she didn't want to be my friend any more. So I'm not lying, if that's what you think,' said Melody.

'Yeah, she's not,' said Theo. 'Violet told her that she didn't want to be friends with someone with bad BO.'

Melody's head dropped.

'It was so terrible what she said,' she whined, 'but what was worse was that she said it in front of everyone.'

'Well, now you know how others feel when you say

nasty things to them,' I replied, not feeling a shred of sympathy.

'I really am sorry, Prune,' said Melody. 'And I promise that I'll never be mean to you again.'

I wasn't the type of person to hold grudges and Melody did seem to be genuinely upset, plus this was the second time she'd apologised to me.

'It's all right, let's just move on from it. I forgive you,' I said tentatively.

'You do?' said Melody, sounding surprised.

I nodded.

'And what about you, Doug?' she asked. 'I know I've not been nice to you either.'

And although Doug looked a little unsure, he said, 'I guess if Prune can forgive you, then I can too.'

'Thanks,' she said. Her eyes peered at me timidly. 'When you started here, Prune, I should've given you a chance. And maybe had I not been friends with Violet and Kirsten, then we could've been friends.'

Melody gave me a small smile, but I simply shrugged.

'So we just have two Vile-lets now to put up with,' said Doug once Melody had wandered off, his voice sounding kind of relieved.

'Yeah, and hopefully it means we'll have less vileness coming our way,' I said, really hoping that would be the case.

* * *

My next lesson was maths, and as everyone filed into the classroom, I heard Violet tell Melody that she didn't want her sitting next to her. And I suppose I felt a little sorry for her. Melody went and spoke to Mr Novak, and even though the class was noisy, I knew she was telling him that she'd fallen out with Violet and was asking to sit elsewhere.

'All right, you can sit over there,' said Mr Novak blandly, pointing to my table – not that there was any space, and it meant we all had to shuffle around while Melody brought over her chair and plonked herself down next to me.

'I do hope, Prune, we can be friends at some point,' she whispered as I took out a pencil from my pencil case.

'Yeah, maybe,' I replied, giving her the briefest of smiles.

Melody might've seemed like a changed person, but I wasn't sure I was ready to rush into a friendship with her just yet.

'Right, everyone, settle down,' said Mr Novak. 'So are you all looking forward to today's test?'

Almost everyone responded with a groan.

I for one hated tests, especially maths tests, considering maths was my least favourite subject. The only person who seemed to be happy about the test was Willow.

'Will there be a prize, Mr Novak, for the person who gets all the questions right?' she asked him.

Willow had won the prize for our previous maths test – a pencil sharpener – which to me wasn't anything to get excited about, though Willow had been ecstatic.

Mr Novak shook his head. 'No prize today, Willow, but I am still expecting everyone to do well. There should be more than one person who can answer all the questions correctly.'

'I'm a bit nervous about this test,' whispered Melody as Mr Novak started bringing the test round. 'I never like doing tests.'

'Me neither,' I admitted, 'but it's not like it's a major test or anything, so there's no point getting worried about it.'

'You're right,' said Melody. 'Anyway, good luck.'

'Yeah, you too,' I replied gingerly.

'Right then – there are fifteen questions to answer,' said Mr Novak as the test lay face down in front of us, 'and you have twenty-five minutes to complete the test, starting from *now*.'

I turned the test over and was pleased to see that the first question on percentages was super easy. In fact, I was finding all of the questions easy until I got to number seven, a question on fractions. From the corner of my eye, I could see Melody with her arm up and I wondered if she'd already finished. Mr Novak came over.

'What is it, Melody?' he whispered.

'It's Prune, Mr Novak. She's been copying my answers,' she said, loud enough for everyone to hear, and the whole class gasped as they looked at me in astonishment – even Doug and Theo.

'That's not true! I've not been copying her,' I said, feeling more shocked than if I'd been struck by lightning.

'It *is* true, Mr Novak. I saw her,' said Violet from across the room. 'Prune's a cheat!' she added with an evil smirk.

'I didn't cheat, Mr Novak – I didn't,' I said as his eyebrows shot up.

He considered this for a moment before saying, 'I think it might be best if you don't sit next to each other. Theo, can you swap seats with Prune?'

'But why should I have to be the one that moves?!' I blurted. 'I didn't cheat!'

I knew I shouldn't have trusted Melody. She didn't want to be my friend. It had all been a trick to make me look like the world's worst person. That was certainly how she and the other Vile-lets had made me feel.

'Please just do as I say, Prune,' said Mr Novak.

I sighed as I got up. It might've only been the other side of the table I was moving to, but I felt like a criminal on their way to prison.

'Right, kids, after that short *interlude* I want you to

95

all return to the test,' said Mr Novak. 'I'll add on an extra five minutes.'

I didn't even care about carrying on with the test. I felt seriously cross, which made my colour clouds emerge and expand across the room like a beast letting out an almighty roar.

I've never cheated in anything in my whole life and I never would!

I started doing a doodle on the test sheet of the most grotesque-looking worms.

I smiled craftily.

I want there to be real *worms. That'll show them!*

But as I watched my colour clouds coil into a funnel, I quickly changed my mind because I don't like worms that much.

No worms, no worms! I shouted in my head.

But clearly it was all too late, and I could do nothing now to stop my drawing from lifting off the page and disappearing into the funnel. I even tried to pinch it away, but there was only the air between my fingers.

Theo looked up from his test, giving me a curious glance, but to him, I must've looked like I was fiddling with my hands because of course, he couldn't see the colours or what was happening. No one could.

The colours quickly vanished, but – to my surprise – no worms appeared on the table. However, my doodle was no longer on the test sheet, so just where were the worms? Across from me, Melody was twirling her pencil while reading a question on the test. But then her pencil fell to the floor. She bent down to fetch it and suddenly her eyes grew wide with horror as she lifted her hand. She was holding a worm! She screamed, then swiftly tossed it away, only for the worm to land on Violet's head, which made her start screaming too. I laughed and so did everyone else.

'It's not funny!' Violet wailed, her eyes narrowing at all of us.

'Settle down, everyone – settle down,' said Mr Novak as he approached our table. 'What on earth is going on?'

Then suddenly Amber let out a scream, followed by Theo, as they both jumped out of their chairs. I peered under the table, and to my shock, several worms were wriggling beneath it.

'Where did they come from?' said Doug as he looked as well.

'It's an infestation!' cried Melody. 'A worm infestation!'

Instantly the class descended into chaos, with almost everyone – including me – rushing to the front of the room to get away from the worms even though the worms couldn't move very fast.

'Oh, will you all stop fussing! It's only a couple of

worms. They're not dangerous,' said Mr Novak as he scooped up my brought-to-life worms on to a piece of cardboard from the art supplies.

I hoped that was true. I hadn't imagined the worms as being poisonous or radioactive, but who knew? I still had no idea what my power was capable of.

'Though what I'd like to know is who exactly brought these worms inside?' said Mr Novak, his eyes looking questioningly at Doug and Theo. 'I know they didn't just appear out of thin air, and I would hate to think this was some sort of ploy to get out of taking the test.'

The two boys shook their heads.

'Those worms are definitely not mine,' said Theo, his face looking seriously grossed out.

'Right, I'm going to take these worms outside, but I want everyone to just calm down, so please will you all go back to your seats and continue with the test,' said Mr Novak. 'And no mucking about – or cheating – while I'm gone,' he added as he left the classroom.

'They were the yuckiest worms I've ever seen,' said a flustered Willow as we went back to our table.

But I could only nod as I tried my best to not look guilty for creating them. It was now even more important that I found a way to control my power, because I dared not think what could happen if I accidentally brought to life something that was much, much worse.

CHAPTER 17

I couldn't wait to get home to try out my power again, only this time I needed to make sure it wouldn't get out of control. I especially needed to practise making things disappear.

Jesse wasn't home even though Mama had given him strict orders not to leave the house due to his exclusion from school. *Trust Jesse not to listen*, I thought. *I bet anything he's with Bryce.* I called his mobile, but it went straight to voicemail.

I left a message – 'Where are you, Jesse?' – before hanging up.

On the plus side, Jesse not being home did mean I had the place to myself and that I could test my power in peace.

At first, I didn't know what to draw, though I definitely knew I didn't want to draw another scarf.

Just why had it kept growing? I pondered. *And why did the worms appear even after I'd changed my mind?*

I took my sketchbook out of my rucksack and opened it to a fresh page. I needed to draw something simple, at least to begin with. Something that wasn't going to do anything strange or unpredictable. So I decided to draw a new pencil set.

As I drew, I knew I needed my feelings to summon the colours, so I had to think of something that would stir up my emotions. So as I focused on my finished picture, I let my mind remember the day when my dad left, which was one of the saddest days of my life.

Jesse and I had been waiting for him to pick us up from school, and I remember feeling really worried because he was never late. Eventually, it was Mama who turned up and I knew something wasn't right, even though she was smiling and trying to sound upbeat. She drove us to this fast-food place called Shiny Happy Hotdogs. But the hotdog she bought me didn't make me feel happy because I still couldn't stop worrying about where Dad was. And it was only when we'd finished our meal that Mama finally told us that Dad had left, the shock of it all making me puke up my shiny happy hotdog all over the restaurant's shiny wooden floor.

As I recalled this memory, an all-too-familiar gloom swirled in my stomach as the colours began to fill the room.

I wished and wished for the pencil set to come to life, gazing at the colours as they swept the picture up from the page. Then, within a short second, the pencil set appeared. I would've practised making it disappear, but I wanted to keep it as I actually needed some new pencils. I waited a couple of minutes to see if anything weird would happen – like the pencils suddenly growing into gigantic pencils – but thankfully they stayed as ordinary pencils, exactly as I'd drawn them.

I tried them out, drawing another picture, of a key ring shaped like a star. The pencils worked perfectly, and the tips weren't even breaking off as often happened to my other pencils. I'd managed to bring something to life that was even better than my regular stuff!

With this in mind, I promptly scribbled out the picture of the key ring. It felt too basic. Nothing had gone wrong with the pencil set, so maybe nothing would go wrong with anything else.

It was time to really test what my power could do.

I turned to another fresh page in my sketchbook and started to draw a picture of a teacup ride, like one I went on at a funfair two years ago. I wasn't sure what made a teacup ride spin, so I decided to draw a lever that I would use to turn it once it came to life. When I was done, I took my sketchbook out to the garden and summoned the colours again by thinking about the day my dad left us.

He'd rung us from a friend's house and told me and Jesse that he'd see us soon, but sadly we never saw him again, and this memory was enough to make the colours immediately return.

And this time I didn't have to wish for long. Just concentrating my mind on wanting the teacup to be real was all that was needed to have the colours whirling into a funnel. My drawing floated off the page and vanished into it. Then at lightning speed, the teacup ride appeared. The cup was brown, blue and white, with flowers decorating its sides and a saucer beneath it. Exactly as I'd drawn it.

I went up to the ride, opened the gate and sat down in the cup. I pushed the lever forward and the cup began to move, spinning slowly on the spot. I smiled, feeling relaxed and enjoying my view of the garden as the cup went round and round.

Suddenly and bizarrely, the ride began to speed up. I hadn't a clue why it was doing this, so I hurriedly grabbed the lever. But when I pulled it, it didn't do anything to make the teacup slow down. Instead, the teacup just got faster and faster until it was spinning totally out of control!

What had I done?!

CHAPTER 18

I had to get out of the teacup, but I could barely stand. When I tried to, I fell back down as the teacup continued to spin like crazy. Blood rushed to my head as I clung to the sides for dear life. I needed to make the teacup disappear. So remembering how I'd made the scarf vanish, I tried to imagine the teacup disappearing from the garden.

But even as I did this, the teacup stayed right where it was – whirling madly with me inside it – and I was starting to feel sick. I tried to get my mind to focus, but my head was feeling seriously dizzy. I took some deep breaths to compose myself, then once again imagined the teacup disappearing.

Eventually, the teacup vanished and I fell on to the grass with a bump.

In a daze, I picked myself up and went back inside the house, my legs wobbling like a newborn fawn taking its first steps. I lumbered up the stairs to my bedroom and lay on my bed until my dizziness had eased. I just couldn't understand why my power was so haphazard. It was as if the teacup had had a mind of its own just like the scarf.

Was it always going to be like this with things I brought to life? Would they all just end up malfunctioning?

The scarf should've just been a normal scarf … Maybe I shouldn't have rushed the drawing? And maybe I underestimated just how long the scarf would be. To be honest, the drawing looked more like an athletics track than a scarf. So maybe that was the issue.

Perhaps I should've drawn the lever on the teacup with speed settings or – better still – an off button. Well, whatever the reason for the scarf and the teacup not turning out as they should have, I was just going to have to practise using my superpower some more.

I tried to think of something else to bring to life. I would've loved to have brought to life a swimming pool, but I wouldn't want to run the risk of it flooding the house if it turned out to be too big for the garden. Something else that would be cool, quite literally, would be an ice-skating rink. I love ice skating, even though I've only done it a few times and had to skate very, very slowly to avoid tumbling over. Now, I realised an ice rink most definitely wouldn't fit in our garden, but thought it would be great to create one for the community because there aren't any ice rinks in Delmere or in Ocean View.

Thinking about this made me realise there was a lot of good I could do with my power. And that's exactly the type of superhero I would want to be: one who could make people's lives that little bit better.

My mind began to buzz with ideas …

I could bring to life new homes for the people that lived in our old tower block, as the building had a lot of problems. For one reason or another, the lifts were always breaking down, and there were way too many power cuts, I can tell you. Plus, I could bring to life a new set of swings for the playground in Shellwood Park, as the current swings there were very old and rusty.

For Delmere, I could bring to life a basketball court, which I knew Jesse would love, and a cupcake shop, which I thought Mama could run because she's always dreamed of having her own business and she makes great cupcakes. In fact, Mama is great at baking cakes full stop.

Plus, I could bring to life a whole other planet that I could drop Bryce on to so he'd be far, far away from Jesse. And maybe I could bring to life some school friends for my brother so he wouldn't feel lonely and would be able to forget about Bryce altogether …

But after thinking about all the wonderful things I

could make real, I decided instead to bring something very ordinary to life – a pair of sunglasses. As much as I wanted all the things I'd dreamed of, I knew I needed to keep it simple.

To get the colours to appear, I thought about Grandma and Poppa B, and how I would've loved them to have seen my superpower in action, and I started to feel sad that they would never get to find out just how special I was. And it seemed that moment of glumness was all that was needed to have the colours surrounding me as I willed the picture I'd drawn to come to life. Within moments, a pair of sunglasses appeared on the kitchen table.

Very cautiously I tried them on. To my relief, they really were just normal sunglasses. But I needed to see if I could make them disappear, and it was important that I got this aspect of my superpower under control. I concentrated my mind as I imagined the sunglasses vanishing from the table. Then, as quick as a flash, they disappeared.

Next, I drew a picture of a guitar, one that looked like the guitar Keirra Grace has. I've always wanted to learn how to play the guitar, so I already knew it was definitely something I was going to keep, but I had to at least check that I could make that disappear too.

To summon the colours, I thought about my last day at Oak Nolan School. Mrs Hart had presented me with a card that everyone in my class had signed and a box of chocolates that Mama said weren't just any type of chocolate. They were actually very expensive chocolates, but I later gave the whole box to Jesse because I'd felt too upset to eat them. It was awful saying goodbye to Corinne that day and I hugged her for what felt like a lifetime, our faces streaming with tears.

As the colours appeared at the memory, I willed the picture to come to life, then wished for the guitar to disappear. When it did, I repeated this process a few times more, each time the guitar appearing and disappearing like a moving shadow. I also practised trying to stop the guitar from coming to life after I'd already willed it to. I worked out that I needed to do this before the colours turned into a funnel, and I literally had just two seconds to prevent this. I was glad I finally knew how to do this correctly. And soon I was keen to bring something else to life, something more remarkable.

I went upstairs and took down a picture I'd drawn of a peacock that was on my bedroom wall. I summoned the colours, but rather than thinking up a sad memory, I tried to let my mind locate the feelings already inside me, feelings that lurked in the very pit of my stomach, which – to tell you the truth – had been there for a long time, like a pebble at the bottom of a pond.

All of sudden, a plume of colours began to encircle

me. I quickly willed my picture to come to life, and once the funnel had formed and swept away the drawing, a peacock appeared in the middle of my room.

'Wow!' I mouthed, gazing at the magnificent creature.

The peacock's eyes darted about as he surveyed my bedroom, his beautiful tail rustling against the floor.

Then he ran straight out and into the bathroom.

'What you doing, Mr Peacock?!' I said, rushing after him.

But as I approached, he zoomed past me and headed for Mama's room.

'Get down! You can't be in here!' I said as he stood on top of her bed.

I panicked. Mama would be furious if she found out I'd had a peacock in her room, and I sure didn't want to see the look on her face if she were to find any bird droppings. I briskly shooed the peacock away, but as he hopped down, he darted straight past me again and down the stairs to the kitchen.

'Naughty, naughty peacock,' I puffed once I'd caught up with him.

He crowed as his tail fanned out behind him, the feathers bristling in a magnificent display; the turquoise eyes shimmering brightly. It was an incredible sight. Then, bringing his tail back down, the peacock stepped towards me, his eyes gawking.

'Would you like something to eat?' I said, even though I had no idea what peacocks eat.

He crowed again and began to pace about, and something told me he wasn't happy. Then, without warning, the peacock began to chase me. I ran back upstairs while the peacock stood at the bottom, crowing away.

I don't know why I thought it'd be a good idea to bring something to life with a mind of its own. That was another problem I needed to fix.

With my mind focused, I imagined the peacock disappearing, and right away the crowing stopped. The peacock was gone.

Well, at least this part of my power was now feeling easy.

I went back to my room and examined the picture. The peacock was back on the page, but oddly his mouth was open, even though I'd originally drawn him with his mouth closed. I stuck the picture back on my wall in between a picture I'd drawn of me, Mama and Jesse and my prize-winning picture of a dolphin.

Afterwards, I played my new guitar for a bit, but seeing as it was the first time I'd ever played a proper guitar, I didn't sound that good, unlike Keirra Grace, who's been playing the guitar her whole life. I was pleased I was finally getting to grips with my power, only

I couldn't understand why the peacock had turned on me. When I originally drew the picture, I'd made the peacock look friendly.

So did I need to say that I wanted it to be tame?

I let out a frustrated sigh. It felt like there were so many aspects of my power that I needed to remember, from making sure I got the scale of my picture right to not changing my mind at the very last second – and I guess if it's an animal I'm bringing to life, to be sure to specify that under no circumstances do I want it to bite me. But perhaps this was just how real superpowers worked. Not as simple as they look in the movies. I mean, take Superman, for instance. You don't see him having to worry about the technicalities of how he's going to fly. He just does it, naturally. Whereas my superpower felt as complicated as long division. As I squeezed my guitar under my bed, I wondered again how Mama would react once I told her about my power.

Would she be happy for me and think it was the greatest thing she's ever seen? Or would she get all freaked out?

I promptly shook that last thought away. Mama loved me way too much to ever feel like that. And so I came to a decision.

That night I'd definitely tell both her and Jesse about my superpower.

CHAPTER 19

When Jesse finally arrived home, Mama was with him, and I could tell from the looks on their faces something serious had happened. And I knew there'd be no chance I'd get to tell them about my superpower – at least, not tonight.

'Want to know what I've been doing for the last hour?' said Mama. And without giving me a chance to reply, she said, 'Trying to persuade a security guard not to call the police on your brother – that's what.'

I stared at both her and Jesse in shock.

'He, Bryce and his other hooligan friends were caught trying to shoplift from the sports shop in Ocean View. They didn't manage to get away with anything, but they left Jesse to face the music while they made a run for it,' said Mama.

She turned to Jesse, whose head was lowered. 'You should thank your lucky stars that I know the security guard and Howard, the manager. Still, this is the second time I've had to do something like this! Begging people not to get the police involved.'

Mama's voice began to fill with emotion as she choked back tears. 'When are you going to realise, Jesse, that the road you're heading down only leads to one place – prison. Just how many times do I have to tell you this and ask you not to hang around with Bryce? He doesn't care if you get in trouble.' Mama sighed a long and heavy sigh. 'Maybe it's my fault for not keeping a closer eye on you.'

'It's not your fault, Mama – it's Jesse's!' I uttered.

Jesse briefly lifted his head and gave me a crabby look, but I couldn't help feeling cross with him for upsetting Mama again, and that anger lit up around us in an array of colour clouds.

'Do you understand how serious this all is, Jesse?' Mama asked. 'The shop has already said that next time they won't hesitate to call the police. They already suspect that Bryce has stolen from the shop before.'

Was it Jesse's trainers that he stole?

This very thought made my stomach feel queasy.

'You really are on your last warning, Jesse,' said Mama.

'Oh, so what,' he mumbled.

'So what?' Mama spluttered. '*So what?* How dare you speak to me like that! Who do you think you are?!' She waggled her finger at him. 'I'm telling you this right now, Jesse, while you're living under my roof, you will show me respect. Otherwise, you can head straight out the door and not come back – understand?'

I knew Mama didn't mean what she was saying and that she was just angry, but for a minute, the way Jesse glowered at her, I was scared he'd leave and not return – just like our dad. But instead, he sucked his teeth and stormed up to his room, putting his stereo on full blast.

I was upset with Jesse, but I also felt seriously cross with Bryce. He was nothing but a menace, and it was time that someone stood up to him.

But who was that *someone*?

How do you stand up to somebody when you don't feel brave enough to do just that? I had to find a way to use my power to change things for the better.

CHAPTER 20

The next morning I woke up much earlier than usual. Despite everything that had happened with Jesse, I felt full of excitement, eager to draw another picture. Sitting at my desk with my sketchbook and pencils laid out, I began to draw a goldfish, one that looked similar to an old goldfish of ours called Spike, which Dad had bought for me and Jesse when I was four. We only had Spike for a year before he died, Jesse waking up one morning to find him lying at the bottom of his fishbowl. But maybe my new goldfish would get to live forever, seeing that I'd be the one making it come to life.

I carefully drew and coloured in each little scale on the goldfish, and for the backdrop, I drew a goldfish bowl with water, tape grass and a blue-grey statue of a mermaid with her fishtail curled behind her.

Without even needing to think of something sad to stir the colours, I just allowed myself to connect with the feelings deep inside me. Feelings that were a combination of all the emotions I'd been experiencing recently – sadness, fear, hurt and anger.

When the colours emerged as expected, I wished for the goldfish to be real. Obeying, the colours spun into a funnel then prised my picture out of the page. And when the goldfish bowl appeared on my desk, I couldn't stop grinning.

'Y'know, you really do look like Spike,' I said to the goldfish happily. 'I hope you like your new home.'

The goldfish's mouth opened and closed as if he was speaking back.

'*Yes, I do like it. It's wonderful,*' I said in a French accent, pretending it was the goldfish talking back.

My dad could speak some French years ago, but I expect he can speak a lot more now if he's still living in France. He did teach me a bit. I don't remember that much, but I do know how to say 'yes' and 'no' (*oui* and *non*), 'thank you' (*merci*), and I'm able to say 'I like chocolate ice cream', which is *j'aime la glace au chocolat*, and *bonjour, ma belle*, which means 'hello, my lovely', which was how my dad used to greet me whenever he'd pick me up from school.

'And how are you feeling this bright morning?' I asked my goldfish but in English. I didn't know the words for that in French.

'*I'm feeling great! And I must say, it's strange to think that only a minute ago I was just a picture,*' me/he replied.

'*Bon,*' I said, another French word I remembered, which means 'good'. 'I think I'm going to call you Alf, as in Alfred. What do you think?'

'*Bon!*' me/Alf said in a deep voice. '*I like that name very much. Merci!*'

I replied to Alf in Spanish, which I had been learning at Oak Nolan and was keeping up at Maple Lane. I said 'you're welcome', which is *de nada*.

Just then, Jesse stuck his head around my bedroom door. 'Have you seen my black Nike T-shirt?'

I shook my head.

I was surprised to see him up early, considering he didn't have school today as he was still excluded.

'I can't find it anywhere.'

'Have you checked if Mama's seen it?'

Jesse noticed the goldfish bowl. 'Where did that come from?'

'I drew it and it came to life,' I proudly declared.

But Jesse just burst out laughing. I had thought my brother might've been impressed, but he clearly didn't believe a word I was saying.

'You don't half talk some nonsense sometimes, Prune. Look, just tell me where you really got that goldfish from?'

'I drew him – cross my heart.'

I showed Jesse my sketchbook, but he only laughed again.

'The page is blank, Prune.'

'That's because the goldfish came out of the picture and came to life.'

'Don't be ridiculous, and don't think for a second Mama's going to believe you either, but I'll leave it to you to tell her, seeing as it's your stupid goldfish.'

'He's not stupid!' I responded fiercely. 'He's probably got more brains than you. Anyway, I don't remember you calling Spike stupid.'

'I was just a kid then.'

'And you're still a kid now, even if you like to think you're all grown up.'

Jesse snorted.

'Look, you're going to have to return that goldfish to whatever pet shop you got it from. So if I was you, I'd drop them a line. Get it? Drop them *a line*.' Jesse chuckled. 'But you don't have to worry about me telling Mama about your goldfish. I'm happy to keep it a *sea-cret*. And I'm not *squidding* when I say that. Now, I *cod* go on with my jokes but I won't as I've got much *batter* things to do with my time, like singing some *scales* and listening to some wicked *tunas.*'

'Your fish jokes are so not *finny,*' I said, but I couldn't help laughing myself, and Jesse gave me a thumbs up for my joke.

'But seriously, I did bring the goldfish to life just like I brought the popcorn to life the other day, the one you thought I'd made,' I said. 'I know you thought you were just joking that time when you said the optician might discover I have a superpower, but I really do have a superpower, Jesse.'

But my brother just rolled his eyes as his phone began to bleep. He took it out of his trouser pocket and read the text.

'What's happened?' I asked, noticing a look of nervousness grow on his face.

'Mind your own business,' Jesse snapped, his attitude instantly changing, which made me guess it was Bryce who'd texted him.

Jesse put his phone back in his pocket.

'Jesse, those new trainers of yours – they weren't stolen, were they?' I found myself saying suddenly.

'No,' he grunted. 'I've already told you, Bryce bought them for me with his own money.'

'You're lying – I just know it!'

'No, I'm not lying! Bryce showed me the receipt. So he didn't steal them, all right?!'

'You say that when yesterday you were all trying to steal from a shop.'

'We were just mucking about,' said Jesse, like it was no big deal.

'But just how much trouble do you want to get yourself into for Bryce?'

'Stop bugging me about it! Anyway, it'll be you who'll be getting into trouble when Mama sees that goldfish,' Jesse sniped. 'She won't be happy, you know, especially when she realises she'll have to start buying its fish food.'

'I'll *draw* its food,' I said, grabbing my pencils, but Jesse had already left the room.

Before I left for school, I decided to hide Alf in the big gap between my wardrobe and the wall, just for the time being. And when I got home that afternoon, I rushed straight up to my room to tell Alf about my day. And I'm sure he flapped his tail in anger when I told him how awful the Vile-lets had been to me.

In the playground at morning break, they'd shouted 'cheat' at me. I was so upset. But what was worse was having other kids really believing that I had cheated. Oliver and Willow even asked me why I'd done it, and neither looked convinced when I told them that I hadn't. On top of this, I had Oliver asking if it was true I used to cheat in tests at my old school. Apparently, it was why I'd ended up at Maple Lane, because my old school had kicked me out! And it didn't take two guesses to know who was responsible for that vile rumour.

'I've never, ever been a cheat!' I exploded, and it was like my colour clouds erupted too, mushrooming around me as I sprinted off in tears.

I was worried Doug and Theo might've believed the rumour, but thankfully they didn't.

Then later on, after giving me sly looks all day, Kirsten threw an eraser at my head during our maths lesson while Mr Novak's back was turned. She gave me a fake, 'Sorry, Prune,' and tried to make out she was aiming the eraser at Melody, even though Melody was sat at another table.

So I was glad when I finally got home and away from them. But as the evening went on, I still didn't manage to tell Mama about Alf or about my superpower. I don't know why it felt so difficult to tell her. She even asked me if I was still seeing the colours and, when I nodded, she said that Dr Connelly would get it all sorted out. I really wanted to tell her I didn't need an appointment because the colours were actually a superpower, but my mouth just opened and closed like Alf's, with no words coming out.

CHAPTER 21

I was all set to tell Mama about my superpower the next day, only I woke up feeling terrible. I was coughing and coughing and my nose was all stuffy.

'Well, it looks like there'll be no school for you today, sweetheart,' said Mama, feeling my forehead as I lay in bed. 'I'll let them know and I'll give Sal a call to tell him I won't be coming in either.'

Despite being ill, a little bit of me was pleased that I didn't have to go to school as it meant I wouldn't have to endure the Vile-lets. But I couldn't help but worry what other lies they were spreading about me while I wasn't there. I really hoped I could still rely on Doug and Theo not to believe a word they said so they'd still be my friends when I was well enough to go back.

But at least for today, I'd be spared having to see the Vile-lets.

Turns out, I even got to enjoy breakfast in bed, which Mama brought up while Jesse went off to school by himself. Though Mama warned him she'd be calling the school to make sure he turned up.

After breakfast, I squeezed behind my wardrobe and checked on Alf. I took his bowl to the bathroom, replacing the dirty water with fresh, and I gave Alf his breakfast, some brought-to-life fish food, before putting the bowl back in its hiding place.

Afterwards, I went downstairs, and to pass the time, I drew a picture of a zoo in my sketchbook, one without cages, that had an aardvark, a baby elephant, a zebra, a pair of emperor penguins, otters, an orangutan and a koala.

For lunch, Mama made some tomato soup and we ate it together as we watched some TV. Shortly after, she started putting on her jacket.

'I'm going to have to leave you for a bit, Prune. I need to get a couple of groceries as well as get you some cough syrup. You think you'll be OK on your own for a little while?'

I nodded. 'I'll be fine.'

'All right, I promise I won't be long. But if you need me, just call my mobile and I'll come back straight away,' she said before pattering out of the house.

As I heard her car starting up, I looked at my picture of the zoo. I really wanted to bring it to life, but even though I wanted to tell Mama about my superpower, I didn't think she'd be pleased to find a load of animals in our garden on her return. But then I could always make sure they disappeared before she got back. The thought of bringing to life an actual zoo was just too hard to resist. So, with my sketchbook tucked under my arm, I trundled out to the garden and summoned the colours.

Willing a picture to come to life was starting to feel very easy and natural now, but I was taking no chances and made sure to also wish that my zoo animals were tame. The last thing I wanted was for them to cause chaos like the peacock had. The colours promptly got to work as they scooped my picture up from the page, and I started to feel giddy with anticipation at what was about to happen next. Then, as quick as lightning, there they all were in my garden – my animals!

Very carefully I stepped forward until I was standing right amongst them, the otters running about my feet. It was truly the most breathtaking sight, which made me feel like the luckiest person in the world. The orangutan wandered over, wrapping her arms around me.

'Well, aren't you friendly,' I said to her, happy to see she was tame like I'd wished for.

The orangutan clapped and gave me a smile that

made me forget I was sick. I went over to the zebra and tried to stroke him, but he stepped back cautiously.

'It's OK – I won't hurt you.'

He observed me for a minute as if trying to decide whether to believe me, then slowly he approached, allowing me to stroke him.

'Hey, beautiful. I'm Prune,' I whispered, looking at him in awe.

It was hard to believe I was actually stroking a zebra in my garden. Having a superpower was truly the best thing ever! I toddled around with the penguins next, copying their funny walk, but then I had to go over to the aardvark and shoo her away from the flower bed that she was trying to dig up. The koala had climbed to the top of our oak tree. I waved at him, hoping he would come down to meet me, but he seemed happy to stay up in the tree. But it was nice to have the elephant come up to me, and she started tickling my ear with her trunk. I laughed and the elephant laughed too, making a loud trumpeting sound.

'Barbara, Barbara! Did you hear that?'

Oh no!

It was Mr Simons, our neighbour.

'It sounded like an elephant and I think it's coming from next door,' I heard him say.

I couldn't let him see the animals because not only

would I be in trouble, but so would Mama. Not to mention, I'd simply have no way of explaining what the animals were doing in our garden without having to tell Mr Simons about my superpower. And I couldn't possibly reveal that to him when I hadn't even had the chance to tell Mama.

I had to make them disappear.

'I'll miss you all,' I said quietly as I waved goodbye.

The elephant trumpeted again as if to say goodbye back.

'That was definitely an elephant!' Mr Simons's voice blared.

I tried to clear my mind as I imagined the animals disappearing, but they wouldn't vanish and I could now hear Mr Simons approaching the fence!

'No, Barbara, you stay inside – I'll find out what's going on,' he was saying.

My heart drummed in my chest as I tried my hardest to focus on the thought that the animals had gone.

'Where's all that noise coming from?' Mr Simons demanded to know, his head popping over the fence.

My bottom lip trembled nervously. 'Um … um …'

I glanced over my shoulder. The animals were no longer there.

Now that *was close!*

'Well, then?' said Mr Simons briskly.

'It was um … it was me!' I said, thinking fast.

'But it sounded like an elephant.'

'That's because I'm playing an elephant in my school's end-of-year show. It's set in a zoo. My friend Doug is playing a giraffe.'

Mr Simons raised an eyebrow. 'And why is it that you're not in school right now?'

'I'm sick.'

And although I was, I did a very loud cough for dramatic effect.

'Well, I'm sorry to hear that, but I'd be very grateful if you could be a little quieter. I'm trying to watch a film on the telly,' he said. He paused for a moment before saying, 'So I take it you're all settled in?'

I nodded. 'Yes, we are, thank you.'

'As you probably know, me and my Barbara were very good friends with Jean, your grandmother – and with your grandfather too before he passed,' said Mr Simons. Then, weirdly, he started to sniff the air. 'Goodness me, can you smell that? Oh, it's hideous!'

'Um, I can't smell anything,' I said, even though I could smell the faint whiff of something unpleasant.

'I expect it's a blocked drain somewhere,' said Mr Simons. 'Anyway, you take care now,' he added before walking back off, holding his nose.

I went to search out what was causing the smell, my

eyes scanning the garden for the possible culprit. They stopped in front of our oak tree where there was a big pile of elephant dung!

Uh-oh, Mama is going to kill me.

And then I heard her voice.

'Prune! Prune! Where are you?'

She spotted me through the kitchen window and marched out.

'What are you doing out here? You know you're not well and— *Urgh!* What is that revolting smell?' she said, batting her hand in front of her face.

I tried standing in front of the dung to block her view, but it was too late – she'd already seen it.

'What on earth—?' Her face screwed up in disgust. 'How did that get here?'

I didn't know what to say so instead looked down at my feet.

'Well, it wasn't here this morning.' She crossed her arms. 'And of course, it'll be me who has to clean it up when I've only just painted my nails.'

I continued to stare at my feet, my cheeks burning with guilt.

'Right, young lady, inside! You've got some serious explaining to do.'

CHAPTER 22

I followed Mama back into the house, sitting down opposite her at the kitchen table.

'So, are you going to tell me how that mess got into our garden? And what type of animal even did that? It can't be a fox because I know fox poo doesn't look like that.'

I suddenly felt apprehensive again, despite wanting so much to tell Mama about my superpower.

'I'm waiting,' she said, tapping her foot. 'How did that poo get there?'

I took a breath. 'It was me – well, not who made the mess. It was an elephant who did that.'

'Excuse me?' said Mama, her eyebrows furrowing. 'Does this look like the Serengeti? Because around here, we don't have elephants roaming through people's back gardens, so I want the truth, Prune. Now!'

'I drew the elephant, and not only that, I drew a whole zoo and brought the animals to life. Plus I've been meaning to tell you this – I brought to life a guitar and a goldfish. The goldfish is called Alf and he's my new pet,' I explained, my words coming out in a rush.

Mama stared at me for a good long minute then said, 'Are you telling me you've gone and bought a goldfish without my permission?'

'No, I drew him and he became a real fish. What I'm trying to say, Mama, is that I have a superpower.'

She laughed. 'Well, you certainly have a *superpower* to make up great stories.'

'No, it's not a story. I'll go and get Alf.'

I dashed upstairs and collected Alf's bowl from behind my wardrobe and carefully brought it down. I put the bowl on the kitchen counter as Mama looked at Alf swimming round and round.

'However much that goldfish cost is coming straight out of your pocket money, Prune,' she said sternly.

'I didn't buy him. I really did bring him to life, and I can bring other things to life too. Please let me show you. You'll see it's the truth.'

Sitting back down at the table, I quickly drew two bowls of chocolate ice cream in my sketchbook before allowing my feelings to summon the colours.

'Prune, I really don't have time for your—'

'It's about to happen, Mama,' I said as I silently willed the picture to come to life. The colours swiftly coiled above my sketchbook, spinning and pulling the picture from the page.

Mama looked shocked to see the picture had vanished from the book, but before she had the chance to say a word, two bowls of ice cream appeared on the table.

Mama stiffened.

'W-w-what is going on? Th-th-that just c-c-came out of nowhere,' she said, her eyes bulging like Alf's.

'That's because I made them become real,' I said.

'No, no ... things just don't suddenly *appear* like that, nor do pictures just *disappear*,' she muttered, closing her eyes as if expecting the ice cream not to be there once she reopened them. When she did, she pressed her fingers to her temples, her face looking totally baffled.

'I'll draw something else,' I said, realising I'd have to do more to convince her.

I hurriedly drew a bowl of crisps while Mama just sat in silence, her face still gobsmacked. And once I was done, I showed her the picture.

'I'm going to make it come to life now, Mama,' I said before letting my feelings summon the colours again, and when a bowl of crisps materialised in front of us, Mama's eyes widened even more.

I munched on a crisp. 'Why don't you try some, Mama?'

But Mama slid back her chair as if she wanted to be as far away from the food as possible. 'How long have you been … been able to do … whatever *this* is?'

'Since Monday, when I made a hot-air balloon appear at school.'

'You did what?' said Mama, her eyes flashing.

'It was an accident and no one knows it was me.'

'OK … so it started on Monday,' said Mama slowly, and I could see she was trying her best to get her head around it.

'It's all connected to the colours I've been seeing.'

'Is it?' said Mama, her voice becoming a little fretful. 'Now I wish I'd just taken you straight to the doctor after we'd gone to the optician. We still have to wait until next week for your appointment.'

'Actually, Mama, I don't need to see Dr Connelly now. There's nothing wrong with me,' I said. 'I can control when the colour clouds appear, and it's the colours that bring my pictures to life.'

'And are the colours still appearing when you feel upset?' asked Mama.

I nodded.

'Which makes it all sound like it's stress-related,' said Mama, letting out a weary sigh. 'And there was I creating so much upheaval, moving us to Delmere and making you leave all your friends at Oak Nolan.' She put her hand to her forehead. 'I was so focused on our new start that I didn't stop to think about the impact these changes would have on your well-being, especially when you were still grieving for your grandma. Oh, I feel like the worst mother!'

'You're not, Mama, and I'm not stressed, honest,' I said.

Mama went silent for a minute then started to shake her head. 'This just doesn't make any sense. I'm just an ordinary woman. How can I have a daughter with a superpower?'

'So does that mean there isn't anyone else in our family who has a superpower?' I asked. 'I've been wondering if I inherited it.'

'No, sweetheart, you are most definitely the first, trust me,' Mama replied.

'What about my dad – did he have a superpower? Or anyone else on his side of the family?'

'No, your dad definitely didn't have any superpowers, Prune, nor anybody else in his family,' said Mama.

Then with her head to one side, she started drumming her fingers on the table, her face looking like she was trying to work out the world's toughest maths sum.

'Prune, you don't think you might've eaten something you shouldn't have, or gone and got yourself bitten by a radioactive spider?'

'I'm not Spider-Man, Mama!' I giggled, but Mama's face was deadly serious.

'We need to find out how you got this,' she said, 'because people don't just wake up one day and discover they have a superpower. I wish you would've told me about this as soon as the hot-air balloon appeared.' She paused for a moment. 'Prune, I don't think you should be using this power ... and from today, I don't want you using it ever again.'

'But why?'

'Because we *don't know* what it is or how you got it.'

'But I could do so much with my power. I could ... draw us food so you won't need to go shopping, and I could draw you a new car—'

'Nuh-uh. I don't want you using it to get us stuff.' Mama waggled her finger. 'And I sure don't need a new car, thank you very much. I'm perfectly happy with the one I've got.'

'But can't you see, Mama, I could become a superhero. I could help people.'

'Oh stop it, Prune!' Mama snapped. 'You're not a superhero. You're just a kid with some ... condition!'

'You're acting like I'm ill or something,' I said, a feeling of hurt and confusion stirring in me uneasily like hardened porridge.

'I'm sorry, Prune,' said Mama, more gently this time. 'It's just that until we've figured out how you got this *power*, you can't tell anyone, not even Jesse.'

I didn't tell Mama that I'd already told Jesse, despite him not believing me. Instead I said, 'Can you at least let me use my superpower occasionally? I won't do anything bad with it—'

'I don't want you using it whatsoever, Prune! Do you hear me?!' said Mama, getting cross again.

My heart sank. 'But—'

'No buts.'

I was the one who was now angry as I marched out of the kitchen with the colours blazing around me and stomped upstairs, slamming my bedroom door like Jesse does when he's trying to make a point.

How could Mama be so cruel?

My superpower belonged to *me* not her, so *I* should be the one who got to decide what to do with it. And no way was I willing to stop using it when my superpower was literally the best thing to have ever happened to me.

It was all so unfair.

CHAPTER 23

The colour clouds swamped my room like a fog. I'd never felt so cross with Mama and I was none too happy that I wouldn't even be able to show my own brother my super-power. It was like Mama didn't trust me when I had the chance to do so much good, not just for her and Jesse, but for Delmere and Ocean View, the whole country and even the world!

I could draw toy shops for children everywhere, one for every high street, and in *my* toy shops, all the toys would be free. Or I could bring to life thousands of new sweet shops and cupcake shops. In fact, I could bring to life new hospitals, new parks, new libraries, new *anything* that people needed. But because Mama wanted me to keep my superpower a big secret, I couldn't do any of that stuff. I wouldn't be able to help anyone.

For the rest of the day, I said very little to Mama. But she seemed happy not to speak to me either and said nothing when I took Alf back upstairs then brought down my guitar and deliberately strummed it as noisily as I could.

At the same time, I made sure not to pay her any attention when she looked like she was about to puke after cleaning up the elephant dung, which she'd scooped into a bag and put out with the rubbish.

It felt like Mama wanted to forget our conversation had even happened, and pretend that she hadn't just found out her daughter had a superpower.

Instead, she just babbled on about a new pizza Big Sal's was introducing to the menu that was going to have grapes and sardines for the topping. Mama was doubtful it would take off but said Sal wanted to try out some 'experimental pizzas'.

I could tell Mama was afraid I'd reveal my secret to Jesse, especially at dinner. And because Mama and I weren't speaking, Jesse got suspicious.

'Is there something I don't know about?' he said, his eyes shifting between Mama and me.

'No. What makes you think that?' said Mama, biting down on a lamb chop.

'Because you and Prune have hardly said a word to

each other. You might think I don't notice, but I do.' He grinned. 'I have X-ray vision, Mama.'

He started to laugh, but Mama looked downright petrified, while I couldn't work out whether Jesse was being serious or not. Maybe superpowers really did run in our family.

'Please tell me you don't, Jesse,' said Mama disconcertedly.

'Don't what?'

'Have X-ray vision.'

'I wish.' Jesse shot Mama a puzzled look. 'Are you OK, Mama?' Then he glanced at me. 'You're both acting really strange.'

'No we're not,' said Mama, sounding annoyed. 'Now just eat up, Jesse, before your food gets cold.'

The next day, I was still feeling a bit unwell, so I didn't go to school again. I spent the first part of the morning watching my DVD of *Aladdin*. But then Mama began to complain I was getting under her feet as I danced and sang along to the film when she was trying to tidy the living room. So I retreated to my bedroom and played my guitar. Then Mama came upstairs and told me I couldn't play it because she wanted to take a nap. It was like I couldn't win!

Feeling bored, I took my sketchbook and pencils and

went downstairs and out into the garden. I began to draw a picture of a treehouse. Even though Mama was against me bringing things to life, she couldn't stop my love of drawing. But as I gazed at my finished picture of the treehouse, which looked so amazing, it felt hard to resist the urge of making it become real. And Mama was still sleeping, so it wasn't as if she'd even know.

I promptly summoned the colours and they wasted no time in working their magic as I willed the picture to come to life. And when it did, I did a little dance as I looked up at my beautiful treehouse! I couldn't wait to run up to our oak tree and climb the ladder to it. Inside, the treehouse had cushions and pretty drapes of different materials and a hammock, which I got into and swung about. I was so loving my treehouse. I drew some more pictures and got so wrapped up in my drawing that I completely lost track of time. At first, I didn't even hear Mama calling me.

'Prune!' she yelled, sounding extremely irate. 'Answer me!'

Eek!

I popped my head out of the treehouse window.

'What is this?' said Mama crisply. 'I told you I didn't want you bringing anything else to life!' she added, but lowering her voice, probably in case the neighbours heard that bit. 'Prune Melinda Robinson, you come down here this second!'

I sighed and went down the ladder, ready to face the music.

'I want you to get rid of this treehouse right away!' said Mama.

I nodded slowly, but it was so annoying that I couldn't keep it. Turning back round, I looked up at the treehouse and muttered a quiet farewell then imagined it gone before it disappeared into thin air. Mama marched me back to the house.

'I want to know why you created that treehouse,' she said when we were safely back inside.

'Because I love drawing, Mama – and, well, the picture I drew looked so pretty that I just wanted to see what it'd look like as a real treehouse.'

'I know how much you love to draw, Prune, but I specifically told you that you weren't to use your super-power. What if Mr Simons had seen that treehouse appearing out of nowhere? Do you know the problems that might've caused?'

'I'm sorry, Mama, but you've got to admit it was a very pretty treehouse.'

'I don't care if it was pretty! I care about you not doing as you're told.'

She shook her head at me.

'Right, I want you to stay in the living room where I can see you. And I want you to give me your sketchbook because right now I don't think I can trust you to keep your drawings as *drawings*.'

'Please don't take it, Mama,' I pleaded. 'I need it.'

'Just hand it over,' she said in an even sterner voice.

I let out a sigh as I gave her my sketchbook, feeling both miserable and cross at the thought of being separated from it. To someone else, it might have looked like a simple sketchbook, but to me, it was a part of who I was. It was like having an extra arm or leg.

I was certainly going to feel lost without it. What was I meant to do now?

CHAPTER 24

When Jesse got home from school, Mama set about making our dinner.

'How's it going?' he said, plonking himself down on Grandma's old armchair.

'Mama has confiscated my sketchbook,' I told him gloomily.

'Why did she do that?'

But of course, I couldn't tell Jesse the real reason, even though I'd already tried to tell him about my superpower, seeing as Mama now forbade me from speaking of it again. But he still probably wouldn't believe me. So instead I said, 'I was cheeky to her and she's still angry with me so won't give it back.'

'Well, maybe she will once she's calmed down,' said

Jesse. 'Still, it's only a sketchbook. If you want to draw something, can't you just use any paper?'

'It's not *only* a sketchbook,' I said, offended. 'It's *my* sketchbook. It has pictures in it that are important to me.'

Even though it had only been a few hours since Mama had taken it away, I was really missing my sketchbook and felt tempted to secretly bring another one to life.

After Mama had put her casserole in the oven, she went upstairs to get changed into her work uniform. She was going to cover the shift of another waitress at Big Sal's.

'I won't be back until very late,' she said when she came down and collected her handbag. 'The casserole should be ready in about two hours. And while I'm not here, I want you kids to be on your best behaviour,' Mama added, looking pointedly at *me* as she said this and not my brother.

Mama left for work, and when the casserole was ready, Jesse and I ate it at the dining table.

'You'll never guess what I found the other day in the cellar,' said Jesse.

'What?'

'Poppa B's cloak – you know, the one he'd wear when he'd tell us a story and would try and act like he was some old, wise wizard?'

I giggled. 'I remember that cloak and I loved Poppa's stories.'

Back when Poppa was still here, whenever Jesse and I would come to stay, he'd always make sure to tell us a bedtime story. They were made-up stories, though he did claim some of them were true. But anyhow, they were all amazing stories even if a few did scare me a little. They'd be stories of kids going on epic adventures, or kids who'd become warriors as they battled to save their kingdom, or kids who'd find themselves having to defend the earth from an alien invasion. And even when Poppa got sick, he still loved to tell us these stories.

I suddenly thought about what Theo had said about the Delmere Magic. Had it been Poppa who'd originally told me that story?

'There's a boy in my class, Theo, who reckons there are kids in Delmere with superpowers,' I told Jesse.

'Yeah, right!' he scoffed.

'It's called the Delmere Magic because the town supposedly has some ancient magic running through it,' I continued regardless.

'As if!' said Jesse derisively.

'I think Poppa B might've told us the same thing. Do you remember him ever telling us about kids having superpowers?'

'No, I don't think he did. But what is it with you

and superpowers all of a sudden? First, you try to convince me that you have one, and now you say your friend reckons there are kids in this town who've got them. It's like you're obsessed, Prune! Seriously, no one in this world has superpowers.'

I could feel the words on the tip of my tongue. *I do*, I so badly wanted to say to Jesse, but the words that quietly slipped from my mouth were, 'I guess.'

After dinner, Jesse and I watched some TV. It was late and I should've already been in bed, but it was nice staying up with my brother, the two of us eating chocolate chip cookies, just like old times.

Suddenly the doorbell rang. I looked at Jesse, my eyebrows rising because who would be ringing our bell at this time? It couldn't have been Mama because she wasn't due home for at least another hour and, besides, she had her keys.

The bell rang again and Jesse got up.

'I don't think you should answer it. We don't know who it is,' I said, but my brother had already headed out to the hallway. I quickly followed and as Jesse threw open the door, my heart thrummed at the sight of the person on our doorstep.

It was Bryce Mackenzie.

CHAPTER 25

'Come in,' said Jesse, as he bumped fists with Bryce.

'What is *he* doing here?' I said.

'Well, isn't that some welcome? Good evening to you too, Prune,' said Bryce sarcastically.

'Ah, take no notice of her,' said Jesse, and like the flip of a switch, his whole attitude changed towards me. 'Just go to bed, Prune,' he hissed.

It was like Bryce had him under a spell; a spell that needed to be broken.

'Our mama doesn't want Jesse having anything to do with you!' I dared to say, though I wasn't sure how I actually found the courage to utter it.

'Seriously, just go to bed,' Jesse growled, his face clouding with anger.

'Yo,' said Bryce, putting his hands up. 'I didn't come here to cause any trouble.'

He pulled his rucksack off his shoulder and held it in front of him as he looked at me.

'I only dropped by to have a little catch-up with my best mate.'

'Well, I don't want you here!' I said boldly.

'Shut up, Pugface!' Jesse flared.

And hearing this made Bryce burst out laughing. 'That name is mad funny, but I can sort of see why you call her that. She does look like a pug, doesn't she?'

Jesse nodded, which made me feel really cross, but what was worse was how he just stood there allowing Bryce to make fun of me.

They both went up to Jesse's room while my colour clouds flamed around me like an erupting volcano. I wish I could've brought to life a giant bumblebee to chase Bryce out of the house and sting him on the bum.

What was Bryce even doing here, and at this time of night?!

No way had he just dropped by. He and Jesse were up to something, and I wanted to know what.

I quietly snuck up the stairs and crept towards Jesse's room. He had his music playing, so I couldn't hear any of what they were saying. I sighed and went to my own room. After a few minutes, I heard Jesse and Bryce come out and head downstairs. I tiptoed back out and stood at the top of the landing.

'Don't forget, I'm counting on you,' I heard Bryce say as Jesse showed him out.

And then at last Bryce was gone.

'Did you know he was coming here? Did you invite him?' I said, coming down the stairs.

Jesse said nothing as he turned round to face me.

'I wonder what Mama's going to say when I tell her how he just showed up.'

'No, Prune – you can't tell her!'

'But you know she can't stand Bryce and would hate it that he was in our house,' I said. 'I really don't know why you're still friends with him, and I bet whatever Bryce has asked you to do is something that'll only get you into even more trouble.'

'He hasn't asked me to do anything,' Jesse retorted.

'And why did you let Bryce make fun of me? Why is it that you always turn nasty whenever he's around?'

'I'm sorry, Prune. I shouldn't have acted like that,' Jesse replied sheepishly. 'It's just …'

'What?'

'Nothing.' He cleared his throat. 'Look, it's late and Mama will be back soon and will be wondering why we've not gone to bed, so if you don't mind, I'm going to go up,' he said sombrely. 'Night, Prune.'

'Yeah, night,' I murmured, but I couldn't help feeling annoyed with Jesse.

A few minutes later, as I was getting ready for bed, I kept thinking about what Bryce had said to my brother as he was leaving.

What exactly was he *counting on* Jesse to do?

CHAPTER 26

Saturday evening arrived, and I was feeling much better, plus I couldn't have been more pleased when earlier in the day Mama finally handed me back my sketchbook. And to top it all, tonight was the night that Corinne was coming to the house for our sleepover.

As soon as she arrived, we both flung our arms around each other.

'It's so good to see you, Prune,' she said.

'And it's amazing to see you!' I replied.

'I hope you girls have a great night,' said Corinne's mum, Daphne, as we waved goodbye and bolted up to my bedroom.

On the floor, I'd laid out some snacks – crisps, Skittles and some cookies. But the first thing I did was show Corinne Alf.

'He's so sweet,' she cooed. 'When did you get him?'

'A few days ago,' I said and wondered how Corinne might react if I told her about my superpower. I'd told Mama I wouldn't tell anyone else, though I'd never kept a secret from Corinne before.

'Your house is so nice and I love your room,' she beamed as we plopped ourselves down on my rug. 'I've got so much to tell you, Prune,' she said and began to tell me how her parents were planning on taking her to Disney World for their summer holiday, which she was 'counting down the days to'.

And according to Corinne, my old school was still the same, and their end-of-year show was going to be *The Wizard of Oz*.

'And I'm playing Dorothy!' she exclaimed.

'That's great! I'm really pleased for you, Corinne.'

'We don't have long to rehearse though. At first, Mrs Kingsbury refused to even let us have a show. I think it had something to do with Lucas Miller's brother setting off the fire alarm during last year's production. But I think once she realised how much everybody wanted a show, she changed her mind.'

Corinne ate a cookie.

'I was really worried I wouldn't get the part as I didn't think my audition went that well. But when I found out I did get it, I was so, so happy. Mrs Hart's dog,

Burt, is going to be playing Toto. I haven't met him yet, but she says he's very well-trained. And my mum is making my costume.'

She took some crisps. 'So, what's been happening with you? Did the optician say you need glasses because of the colours you were seeing?'

'No, my eyes are fine.' I paused for a second. Looking at Corinne, it didn't feel like it would be as hard to tell her about my superpower as it had been telling Mama. 'Actually, the colours are to do with something else. But before I tell you, you need to promise you won't tell anyone else?'

Corinne nodded and then we did our special hand-shake where we promise to keep our secrets forever.

I took a deep breath. 'I can bring my drawings to life by willing them to be real. And the colours I told you about – well, they make it happen.'

Corinne just stared at me blankly.

'I know it probably sounds really strange but … I have a superpower, Corinne!'

'I don't get it,' she mumbled.

'I think it might just be best if I show you.'

Although I'd promised Mama I wouldn't bring anything more to life as a way of getting my sketchbook back, I just had to show Corinne my power. So with my sketchbook in one hand and my pencils and imagination in the other, I started to draw a picture of some candy-floss.

Once I was finished, I showed Corinne the picture before placing my sketchbook in my lap as I connected to my inner feelings to summon the colours.

'They're here, Corinne – the colours are here!' I told her as the colours began to surround us: light blue and dark blue, pale yellow, bright yellow, olive green and apple green, cherry red and ketchup red, purple grape and purple plum, and browns the colour of chocolate and maple syrup – not to mention loads of other hues.

'I can't see anything,' she said, her eyes glancing around the room.

'That's because I'm the only one who can see them. But they're everywhere, trust me. Now I need to will my picture to come to life.'

And as I did this, the colours began to spiral as usual above my picture.

'The picture … it's gone!' said Corinne, pointing at the suddenly blank page in my sketchbook, her eyes blinking in amazement.

But when a bag of candyfloss appeared between us, Corinne was even more amazed.

'Where did that come from?'

'It's my picture come to life.'

'But that's impossible,' she uttered.

'Like I said, I have a superpower. I've actually brought quite a few things to life, like a treehouse, my guitar, a hot-air balloon and Alf. He started life as a picture.'

Corinne's eyes grew as big as Mama's cooking pots.

'You drew him and all that other stuff?!'

I smiled. 'Yep.'

Corinne looked truly stunned.

'So is Alf like a ... robot?'

'No, he's a real goldfish.'

Corinne blinked. 'Wow! So this candyfloss, it's real too?'

I nodded. 'Why don't you try it?'

Corinne looked at the bag uncertainly, so I decided to dive in first.

'It tastes like normal candyfloss,' I tried to reassure her, and Corinne carefully scooped some up and plopped it into her mouth.

'It's delicious, Prune,' she said, her voice growing with excitement. 'Make something else come to life, *please*.'

This time I thought I'd surprise Corinne by not letting her see what I was drawing as I summoned the colours again.

'Close your eyes and no peeking.'

She closed her eyes, but when I got up and turned

off the lights, she quickly reopened them and gasped when she saw what was in the corner of the room.

'A Christmas tree!' she squealed.

'And what d'you know, it's not even Christmas.'

The tree was just perfect: not too big and not too small.

Corinne hugged me.

'It's gorgeous, Prune!' she trilled, admiring the tree, which was decorated with tinsel, silver baubles and fairy lights.

No one loved Christmas more than Corinne. She loved it to the extent she would put her stocking out in October just in case Santa decided to make an early visit.

'And there's a present under it,' she burbled, walking over to the tree and picking up a box in gold wrapping paper.

'It's for you,' I said. 'Open it.'

Corinne pulled off the wrapping then lifted the lid off the box.

'It's a pair of rollerblades!' she gushed, taking them out.

I knew Corinne had wanted rollerblades since forever, but her parents weren't too keen on buying her a pair. The rollerblades were in her favourite colours too, purple and yellow.

'I love them! But for now, I think I might have to

hide them from my mum and dad. I'm not sure they'll want me wearing them. So I'll have to skate in secret. Still, I can't wait!' Corinne put them back in the box. 'Your superpower is so awesome, Prune. But, what if you don't want to keep the thing that you've brought to life? Because that tree is probably going to start shedding soon, and by Christmastime, it won't look so nice.'

'All I need to do is imagine that it's not there and it just disappears,' I said simply.

'But if things can easily disappear, does that mean I'll wake up one morning and my rollerblades will be gone?' asked Corinne.

'No, they should last forever, providing you take good care of them.'

'So even if they get wet or something, they won't just suddenly dissolve?'

I shook my head. 'No, that won't happen.'

I took one of the baubles off the Christmas tree and poured a little water on it.

'See! This hasn't disappeared,' I said.

I showed Corinne my guitar next and she had a play.

'I wish I had a superpower,' she said.

'What kind of superpower would you want?' I asked.

'I'd love to be able to read people's minds, because that way I'd know what presents my parents were planning to get me every birthday and Christmas.'

'Yeah, that would be a cool ability,' I agreed.

But then I thought of the Vile-lets. I don't think I'd want to read their spiteful thoughts.

'And it would be great to be able to travel through time,' said Corinne. 'That way I could travel to the future to see if I become a famous actress.'

'I've been wondering if there might be other people who are like me,' I said, eating some more of the candyfloss.

'My friend Theo reckons there have been kids in Delmere who've developed superpowers all because of some ancient magic. He said his gran knew a boy who could fly.'

'Really?!' said Corinne, astonished.

I shrugged. 'He could've been pulling my leg. But the more I think about it, the more I feel like I've heard the story before, but I can't remember where. But the thing I don't get is why didn't I have this power before? And how comes I have it and not every kid? So that makes me wonder if there really is some hidden magic in this town.'

'And what does your mum think? Does she know about your superpower?' asked Corinne.

I nodded slowly. 'She knows, but she wants me to keep it a secret – that's why you can't tell anyone. She doesn't even want me to use it. It's like she thinks my superpower is something bad.'

'But it's good because you could do so many brilliant things with your power, Prune!'

'I know and I tried to tell her that, because then I could help her, Jesse and people everywhere. I could become a superhero, Corinne!'

'Yeah, with your own superhero name and superhero costume. How amazing would that be?' she replied excitedly.

'So amazing! And I wouldn't even have to make my costume because I could just draw one and bring it to life!'

'Oh, Prune, I can't tell you how great it is having a best friend with a superpower,' said Corinne with a huge smile.

'So, what shall we do next?' I said, popping some Skittles into my mouth.

'Listen to some Keirra Grace?' Corinne suggested.

'Yeah, let's do that.'

So we spent the rest of the evening singing along to Keirra Grace songs and playing my guitar until it was time for us to go to sleep.

CHAPTER 27

On Monday it was time for me to return to school. We dropped Jesse off on the way, and Mama pulled up outside my school gates. Just as I was about to get out of the car, she turned round in her seat to face me.

'Prune, I did a bit of research on the internet to see if I could find anything on ordinary people having superpowers. But sadly, I found nothing. So it appears what you have is totally unique. And, sweetheart, I know you're probably finding all of this exciting, but it's important that your *special ability* just stays between us.'

For a moment I considered confessing that I'd told Corinne, but knowing it would probably make Mama angry, I decided to say nothing.

'I love you so much, Prune, and all I want to do is

keep you safe,' said Mama before giving me a kiss goodbye.

Doug seemed pleased to see me back at school, and it was good to see him too, as well as Mrs Downing, who had also returned after her sickness. But it wasn't good seeing the Vile-lets, who were being their usual horrid selves.

When I was speaking to Theo and Doug in the play-ground during morning break, they rushed over blaring in unison, 'Prune's infected, and if you don't stay away from her, you'll catch what she's got!' before running off with their hands covering their faces as if to shield them-selves.

Then at lunchtime, having made sure no teachers were looking, Violet deliberately tripped me up, sending me head first into my plate of macaroni cheese. I felt so embarrassed and was trying my hardest not to cry as Doug helped me up and gave me a napkin to clean the goo off my face. The Vile-lets had completely ruined my day, and when I got home I was still feeling down-beat. I went to make myself a snack – a peanut butter sandwich – but I couldn't eat it, a hollow feeling gnawing at my stomach.

Why were the Vile-lets so intent on making my life a misery?

I started to think of things that would make me feel

better. Returning to my old school would definitely help. So would getting to permanently wipe the smirks off the Vile-lets faces. But within that moment, the thing I felt myself wanting the most – what I knew would completely take my blues away – was my dad. I wanted to hear his voice again – hear him tell me that everything was going to be OK like he used to whenever I scraped my knee or became upset because I couldn't find my favourite crayons.

I could draw him, I suddenly thought. *Make him real.*

And all I'd need to do was wish for it to be really *him*. There were no issues with handling my power now, so it should all work.

I quickly grabbed my sketchbook and took the framed picture of Dad off the living room mantelpiece. I started drawing him exactly how he looked in the photo, wearing a red shirt, jeans and clean white trainers. After a short while, I was done, but then I hesitated.

What if Dad decided he didn't want to be back with us? Might he leave again?

I guessed I would just have to do my hardest to convince him to stay.

I inhaled a breath as I summoned the colours.

Finally, my dad was coming home.

CHAPTER 28

As my dad stood in front of me, I literally had no idea what to do. Ever since he'd left, I'd pictured this moment, what I'd say and do. There were times when I'd imagine myself running into his arms, and other times where I imagined myself shouting my head off at him for leaving us. But I didn't do either of these things. Instead, I bolted out of the living room, my heart racing like a train because I simply couldn't believe that it was really him. It had been what I wanted, but somehow I didn't feel ready for it.

When he left us, for ages I was convinced it was because he'd stopped loving me and Jesse, despite Mama always saying that our dad would continue to love us 'to the end of the universe and back', the same thing he used to say when he'd tuck me in at night. But a part of me never quite believed her, especially as Dad never bothered to get in touch, and it's not as if that would've been impossible, considering Mama has the same mobile number that she's always had, a number that's even older than me.

I stayed in the hallway for several minutes, still trying to get over my initial shock. When I found the courage to return to the living room, Dad was standing in the same spot, but he looked sort of confused.

Wasn't he excited to see me? Or maybe he didn't understand why we were in Grandma Jean's house.

Dad's face, though, was just how I remembered it. His forehead was high like mine, and his lips were round like Jesse's. I didn't feel nervous any more and threw my arms around him.

'It's so good to see you, Dad.'

He patted me on the back.

'Have you missed me?' I asked, looking up at him.

He smiled. Well, sort of. The corners of his lips were only turned up a little, so it was hard to tell if he was as happy as I was.

'Have you?' I asked again. 'Because I've missed you, loads.'

'Missed ... missed,' he said, and I hugged him tighter. It felt so good to hear him say that.

I imagined, like me, Jesse would be thrilled to see him, though I wasn't certain how Mama would react. Although she'd never admit it, I think she does miss him. She still likes to play their favourite song, which always makes her eyes go all watery. So maybe she'd ask Dad to stay.

'Promise me, Dad, that you won't leave us again,' I said.

I looked at Dad hopefully, but he didn't look like he was ready to make any promises just yet, his lips staying firmly closed like they were fixed together with cement. But I didn't let this bother me as I was sure I'd win him round.

'We should do something fun,' I said cheerfully and chewed my lip as I tried to think of something. 'How about we go to the park? You used to like taking me to the park when I was a little girl. Do you remember, Dad?'

'Park,' he responded slowly.

'Yeah, shall we go?'

'Park,' he said again.

'There's a park not far from here. We could go there now if you like.'

Dad somehow seemed lost for words. But he seemed happy enough to go to the park, so we left the house together, him holding my hand just like old times.

As we walked, I began to tell Dad everything. He listened and listened but didn't speak, and I figured it was because he just wanted to hear all about me. But I suppose we did have a lot to catch up on. I told him that we were now living in Grandma and Poppa B's old house (just in case he didn't recognise it) and that Mama had a new job and that Jesse and I were both going to new schools, which neither of us liked. I told him all about the Vile-lets, and just how vile they were. It felt good to finally get off my chest how they'd been making me feel.

Dad listened intently, so I continued. I told him that I still loved to draw … Then, throwing caution to the wind, I told Dad about my superpower and some of the things I'd brought to life – the hot-air balloon, the peacock, the zoo, the treehouse and Alf. I just sort of blurted it all out, but unlike when I first told Mama, Dad didn't seem alarmed at all. He simply nodded his head and squeezed my hand a little, something he used to do to show that he was proud of me.

'Alf looks exactly like Spike, Dad. Do you remember Spike?' I said delightedly.

Dad said nothing, so I assumed he didn't remember him.

Fern Park is only a ten-minute walk from our house. It's a nice big park that has a tennis court, but that day there were just a few elderly people sitting on benches and a few parents with their kids in the children's playground. There was a woman with two children who were playing in the sandpit, and another lady whose little boy was on the slide. She smiled at me and Dad. I smiled back, but Dad didn't. I got on a swing and Dad sat on another. I began to swing and Dad copied, but while I was enjoying it, Dad didn't look like he was.

'Dad, do you have a superpower?' I asked.

Even though Mama had said he didn't, I thought I'd ask anyway, to make sure. But Dad stayed silent, which I took as meaning that he didn't have a superpower.

'Do you remember the time when you took me and Jesse to the circus?' I said to him.

Dad nodded, though I couldn't be sure if the nod meant that he did remember.

'I was five and we had so much fun. I can still remember the clowns and the tightrope walker who made everyone gasp when her foot came off the tightrope. Do you remember that, Dad?'

Dad nodded his head more firmly this time.

'Yay! You do remember!' I said, feeling ever so happy.

It really was amazing to have my dad back.

CHAPTER 29

After spending around twenty minutes in the park, I realised that Jesse would probably be home already, and I couldn't let him miss out on reuniting with Dad.

'We should go back,' I said, and as Dad and I walked home, I decided I'd try and find out what he'd been up to in the years since I'd last seen him.

'Is it true that you're living in Paris?' I asked.

'Paris,' he replied.

'So can you speak a lot of French now? *Oui? Non?*'

'*Oui.*'

'That's good. Do you think you'd be able to teach me some more French like you did when I was little?' I asked.

'*Oui,*' said Dad again.

'Great!' I responded cheerily. 'Dad, have you ever been to the Louvre? I'd love to go there.'

'*Oui*,' he said.

'When I grow up I want to become an artist and hold exhibitions all over the world, including at the Louvre. Will you come to my exhibitions, Dad?'

He gave me a dubious look as if he wasn't comfortable replying to that question, but I was sure he would come now that we were back in each other's lives.

When we reached home, Dad looked uncertain about coming in. He kept stepping in with one foot before pulling it out again as he stood on the doormat.

'It's OK,' I said, trying to put him at ease. 'And if it's Mama you're worried about, she won't be in until later.'

My dad sure was acting odd, but I put it down to nerves. I called out to Jesse, but he wasn't in and I really hoped he wasn't somewhere with Bryce. But rather than worrying about my brother, right now I just wanted to focus on spending time with Dad.

'Would you like a Pepsi?' I asked him as we went through to the living room.

I remembered the drink being my dad's favourite.

'Pepsi,' he muttered as he stood in front of the sofa as though waiting for my permission to sit down.

'Cool. I'll go and get you one.' And I headed off to the kitchen.

I took a can out of the fridge, opened it and brought it back to him. I sat down and Dad copied, sitting up straight as he held his drink. Back when I was little, Dad would've sat right back, his body practically moulded into the sofa with one leg balanced on top of the other. As hard as it was for me to admit it, my dad had changed. For one, he used to be a lot more talkative.

'He's much bigger now,' I said to Dad as his gaze rested on a photo of Jesse on the mantelpiece. 'He was eleven in that photo. He's fifteen now and he's as tall as you. I'm not sure where he is right now, but hopefully he'll be home soon and you'll get to see him.'

'Home soon,' said Dad.

'Yes, Jesse is going to be home soon.'

'Jesse,' he said, like he was hearing the name for the first time.

Dad really was behaving awfully strangely.

'Aren't you going to drink your Pepsi?' I asked. 'I could always get you something else if you like. We've got some orange juice.'

'Orange. Juice.'

So I went to get him a glass of orange juice, and Dad looked so silly the way he was holding the can of Pepsi in one hand and the juice in the other. And for a split second, I wondered if he was playing a practical joke, which would've explained why he was behaving so bizarrely.

I remembered how he liked to play pranks on Mama. Like when he'd make out that he'd lost his voice, and sometimes not speak to her for days; or when he'd hide the car keys, meaning she'd have to walk to work, which would cause her to be late.

At least I think they were pranks.

I remember Dad once saying to Jesse, 'Your mum knows I'm just messing about,' when Jesse asked why he'd hidden Mama's purse. And I remember Mama not looking too happy about it but agreeing that it had all been a prank.

'Your dad's just being silly,' she'd said to my brother, 'so there's nothing for you to worry your pretty little head about.'

'Why don't I get rid of these for you?' I suggested, taking the Pepsi and orange juice from his hands and putting them on the coffee table.

But Dad didn't even react. He just stared straight ahead.

'I don't think Mama likes me having a superpower,' I began to tell Dad as I sat back down. 'She doesn't want me using it and says I'm not to tell anyone.'

'Not. Tell. Anyone,' said Dad, his voice as flat as a busted tyre.

Was my dad even interested in what I was saying?

'Do you think you and Mama would ever get back

together, Dad?' I asked him tentatively. 'I do think she still really cares about you, even though she'll act like she doesn't.'

'Doesn't, doesn't, doesn't,' he repeated.

I looked at Dad in bewilderment.

What was up with him?!

Then suddenly my throat felt tight.

'Dad, do you know who I am?' I said, standing up again.

'Who I am? Who … I … am?' he answered robotic-ally, his eyes as blank as a piece of paper.

That's when it finally hit me – my dad had no memories whatsoever and was repeating what I was saying because he wasn't my dad at all. He wasn't real, not *really*. I'd just been fooling myself that he was.

'Dumb drawing,' I muttered, but 'Dad' just carried on gazing ahead.

'Are you even listening?' I shouted through gritted teeth. 'You're not my dad!'

I felt both angry and upset for bringing my picture to life, and those feelings raged around me in a sea of colour clouds.

'I said, *You're not my dad!*'

'Not. Dad,' he shouted back, and hearing him repeat these words felt like a punch to the gut.

But he was right. He was no more my dad than a

clothes shop mannequin. I screamed, but it faltered into a yelp as tears plummeted down my face. My real dad would've comforted me, whereas all this *fake* could do was stare at me with his empty eyes and weird half-smile.

'Go away, go away, go away!' I kept yelling until 'Dad' was gone.

I'd made him disappear just like he'd decided to do himself all those years ago. And as I began sobbing huge noisy tears, I stormed off to the kitchen with the picture I'd drawn of 'Dad'. Furiously, I ripped it into pieces then threw them in the bin along with any hope I once had of ever seeing my real dad again.

CHAPTER 30

'Hey, sis, what's wrong?' said Jesse when he got home a little later to find me slumped on the sofa.

Although I'd stopped crying, I was still upset.

'Where have you been?' I bleated as he sat down next to me. 'I thought you would've been home ages ago.'

'I've joined an after-school computer club. But don't worry about that – I want to know what's upsetting you.'

I still so badly wanted to tell Jesse about my super-power, and for him to finally *believe* me and not think I was crazy, even though I was beginning to hate it. I mean, what was the point of me even having a super-power if it couldn't give me back my dad? Plus, nearly everything I'd created I'd had to say goodbye to, whether that was my treehouse, the zoo or even the Christmas tree I brought to life for Corinne. It's like my whole life has been a big spinning teacup ride of me having to say goodbye, made more painful when those goodbyes have been to those I love. And I was beginning to realise that whatever I brought to life could never truly be *real*.

So instead of telling my brother how I'd brought to life a fake Dad, I confessed that I was being bullied. I told Jesse everything – about the name-calling and how the Vile-lets had accused me of cheating in the maths test and started a rumour about me getting kicked out of my old school, and how Violet had deliberately tripped me up. And once again, I felt a great sense of relief at being able to talk about how miserable they'd left me feeling.

'You can't let them get away with this, Prune,' said Jesse adamantly.

'But what can I do?'

'Well, have you thought about telling Mama?'

'No, I don't want to tell her.'

'But she could speak to your teacher if you don't feel like you can do it yourself.'

'Well, I suppose I could tell Mrs Downing,' I said slowly.

'You should, Prune,' said Jesse. 'Bullies are very good at targeting people who they think are weaker than them. I should know, seeing as I was bullied myself once.' He looked at me thoughtfully. 'But one way you can handle them, Prune, is to stand tall, and try not to be scared no matter how hard that might feel.'

I nodded gingerly.

'Though I can totally see why you call them the Vilelets. They really do sound like a vile bunch of girls.'

'My friend Doug came up with that name. They've been picking on him as well.'

'Just remember, sis, it's them who have the problem, not you. And no doubt there isn't anything special about them, but you're special, Prune.'

For a second I wondered if Jesse finally believed that I had a superpower. Maybe Mama had decided to tell him she'd seen the proof for herself.

'What with your talent for art,' he continued. 'I'm expecting huge things for you, sis. But just don't you go forgetting me when you're all rich and famous, you hear?'

He gave me a playful nudge.

'I won't,' I said softly. 'But I'm sure you'll be rich and famous as well.'

'Hey, I've got a joke for you,' said Jesse, and I knew it was his way of trying to cheer me up. 'What do elves do when they get in from school?'

I shrugged.

'Their *gnome*work of course!'

'OK, that's a good joke,' I said.

'Glad you like it, but where's that smile of yours gone, because I know it's there somewhere?'

Slowly, I curved my lips into a smile.

'There it is!' Jesse grinned.

But smiling did make me feel somewhat better. And even though Jesse could annoy me rotten sometimes, it was moments like this that reminded me how much of a great brother he was.

'Now, how about I make us a strawberry milkshake?' he said, getting up and going to the kitchen.

'Yes, please,' I replied, my smile broadening as I followed him in.

'By the way, what time do you normally feed Alf?' asked Jesse, taking the milk out of the fridge.

'Why do you want to know?' I replied, raising an eyebrow.

Jesse shrugged. 'I'm just curious, that's all.'

'But you don't like goldfish. You think they're stupid.'

'Well, maybe they're not completely stupid,' said Jesse. 'I mean, they'll never be able to do tricks like a dog can, but they do make a lot of people happy, so I guess that makes them kind of cool.'

'Well, Alf makes me feel happy.' I paused for a second. 'I don't mind sharing him, y'know. He can belong to both of us.'

'I'm cool with that.'

'Good, because it'll be his dinner time in about five minutes and it's your turn to feed him.'

Jesse let out a groan but smiled. 'Now how did I know you were going to say that? But I suppose feeding him is much better than having to clean out his bowl.'

'Oh, thanks for reminding me, because you're going to need to do that too,' I said with a giggle.

An hour later, Mama arrived home, but I waited until Jesse was up in his bedroom before I told her how I didn't want to have a superpower any more.

'It's useless and it's horrible,' I said to her.

Automatically, Mama got up and closed the living room door. I think she was worried Jesse would hear, not that he was going to over the loud music he was playing.

'Have you been using it again, even though I told you not to?' said Mama, her eyes narrowed.

'No,' I lied. 'I just wish I never had it in the first place, and I wish I could get rid of it,' I said in a bleak voice.

'I'm sorry you feel so upset, Prune, but I wouldn't know if your superpower is something you can get rid of. I imagine it's just a part of who you are,' she said. 'But there is something you can do to make sure it doesn't bother you, and that's not to use it.'

'But I don't want to anyway because I hate it!' I uttered and began to sob.

'Oh, sweetheart, don't cry,' said Mama softly.

She stroked my hair.

'It's funny how I grew up believing superpowers only existed in comics, films and on TV shows,' she said. 'Never would I have imagined that I'd have a daughter who could bring things to life. I've always known you were gifted, but now you're extraordinary.'

She chuckled lightly. 'I suppose what I'm trying to say, Prune, is you have something that there most likely isn't a cure for, so all you can do is to try and cope with it the best you can. And even though I'm not keen on you using your superpower, it shouldn't be something that you hate.'

Mama pulled me into a hug, which felt so soothing, just like all her hugs do.

And I guessed Mama was right. I shouldn't hate my superpower, not when it was something that made me unique. It had brought me Alf, for one, and my beautiful treehouse, even if I did only get to spend a short time in it. And I suppose the colours were always amazing to look at. They certainly made the world feel a lot more vibrant.

But my superpower had also brought me heartbreak, and right now I didn't want to use it ever again.

CHAPTER 31

The following day I was chatting to Doug about the kinds of superpower we thought would be cool to have, like being able to shrink or become huge like Ant-Man or move as fast as the Flash or have supersonic hearing or the ability to make ourselves invisible. Doug admitted he wished he could be invisible whenever the Vile-lets were around. His face drooped sadly as he said this – then, to make matters worse, minutes later we were ambushed by them.

'*Dorky Doug, Dorky Doug. He's the dorkiest Doug there is,*' their voices sang, as they followed us around the playground. It made me so cross they were upsetting Doug as he walked with his head down.

Unable to keep my fury in, I spun round to face them.

'Why can't you just leave him alone?' I spat, which not only surprised Doug, whose eyes widened as he raised his head, but surprised me too. If you'd have told me that morning what I was going to do, I wouldn't have believed it. But I just couldn't watch them being unkind to Doug – the only person who'd always been there for me at Maple Lane.

'Hey, Dorky, is Prune your girlfriend?' Violet crowed as his cheeks went bright red.

'For your information, we're FRIENDS!' I roared. 'So why don't you just buzz off, you vile idiots!' An assortment of colours exploded around me – orange, mauve, cyan, jade, indigo, yellow and teal, amongst others.

As Doug and I strode off, the Vile-lets started to go 'wooooooh' sarcastically, but for a few minutes, I felt pleased that I hadn't cowered and was proud that I'd been able to stick up for Doug. But very quickly I began to have a feeling that I'd only made things worse for myself.

'That was so cool what you said to them,' said Doug, his cheeks still red as we sat down on a bench. 'You're the first person who's ever stuck up for me like that. Not even Theo has, but I think he's scared they'll pick on him too.'

'Doug, I think we have to tell Mrs Downing,' I said. 'They're bullies, pure and simple, and if we don't say anything, they won't stop.'

'I know,' Doug replied quietly. 'I've wanted to tell her for ages. But I guess I've just felt too afraid.'

'Well, you won't have to be any more once I've spoken to Mrs Downing,' I said.

'I erm … saw what happened with Violet, Kirsten and Melody,' whispered Amber to me when we were back in the classroom. 'They were really cruel.'

'It's not the first time they've been like that to me or Doug – or had you not noticed?' I answered stiffly.

'I have,' muttered Amber. 'I saw when Violet tripped you up and I've heard the names she and the others have been calling you.' Amber went quiet for a minute then said, 'I know we haven't spoken much recently, but I wish there was something I could've done to get them to leave you alone.'

'So why didn't you?'

Amber shrugged feebly. 'Well, it would've been three against one, wouldn't it, if they'd decided to come after me.'

'I'm going to tell Mrs Downing what they've been doing,' I whispered.

'Good. All three of them are just awful, especially Violet,' she replied. 'She's what my mum would call a toxic person, and it's best not to have any toxic people in your life.'

'Oh, she's certainly toxic,' Doug interjected. 'All three of them are. In fact, I think they should all walk around with a sign saying, *Warning: Seriously Toxic – Do Not Go Near!*'

'I really am sorry, Prune. Can we start again?' said Amber.

I took a minute to think about it.

I nodded. 'OK.'

'Thank you,' she said gratefully.

'I'm glad you made up with Amber,' Doug whispered during our history lesson. 'Y'know, Prune, you're one of the nicest friends I've ever had. I'm really glad you came to this school.'

I smiled because for the first time since I'd started at Maple Lane, I was actually happy to be there and have Doug as my friend.

Sadly, though, it turned out I was right about making things worse for myself, because at the end of school, the Vile-lets seemed determined to get their own back.

I'd gone to the girls toilets and found all three of them already in there, and straight away they'd swarmed around me like wasps.

'What d'you want?' I said, sticking up my chin and standing tall like Jesse had told me to do. I wanted them to see that I wasn't going to be intimidated.

'Nobody calls us idiots, Alienhead,' said Violet, stepping right up to me, and before I could even think of how I was going to get myself out of this situation, she had dragged my rucksack off my back.

'Give that back!' I said as she opened it.

She took out my sketchbook then threw my rucksack over to Kirsten, who threw it to Melody as if it were a ball.

'Yuck! These pictures are *so* revolting,' said Violet, flicking through the sketchbook. 'Even my little sister can draw better than this, and she's only four.'

She showed the other two, who laughed mockingly.

'And what's this hideous thing?' she said, turning to a picture of a warthog.

I didn't respond. Instead, I gave her a fiery look.

'I think it might be a self-portrait,' spouted Kirsten as the colour clouds began to bloom around me again.

'Yeah, I think you're right,' said Violet, giving me a dirty look. 'Well, here's what I think of your grotty drawing.' She ripped the picture out.

'No!' I shrieked and went to grab my sketchbook, but Melody and Kirsten pushed me back against the wall.

Violet threw the picture to the floor and stamped on it. She then tore out another picture.

'Stop!'

She took no notice as she scrunched the picture into a ball and threw it at my head.

'Please just give it back!'

'Aw, she wants her sketchbook back,' said Violet. 'Sure, I'll give it back. I'll give all your pathetic pictures back.'

She started tearing out more pages, scrunching them into balls and tossing them into the sink, and all I could do was watch helplessly as Melody and Kirsten kept me pinned to the wall. All the while I was wishing for someone to come in and rescue me and my pictures. But no one came. The next thing I knew, Violet had turned on the taps, soaking my drawings.

'How could you!' I yelled, but Violet just laughed.

Finally, Melody and Kirsten let me go. I wanted so much to grab Violet's head and dunk it into the sink, but I quietly picked up my rucksack and went into one of the cubicles, tears stinging my eyes.

'Do you think she might be crying?' said Kirsten.

'Oh, we're *so sorry*, Alienhead,' said Melody, but I knew she wasn't sorry whatsoever.

Anger rumbled through me as I hurriedly fished out my four-colour ballpoint pen from my rucksack and quickly drew a picture of the Vile-lets on the toilet wall.

I had promised myself not to use my superpower again, but the Vile-lets had gone way too far this time.

'We'll give back your sketchbook, but only if you

admit that you're an alien-headed loser,' snorted Violet, kicking the door.

I clicked the pen to make it green then drew slime that completely covered their bodies until you could only see their feet.

'Come on out, Alienhead,' Violet jeered.

But I refused to let her distract me as I concentrated on making the slime come to life.

And not a moment too soon, the Vile-lets started screaming as something splattered down from above.

'Eugh, my hair!' Kirsten howled.

'Eugh, my shoes!' screeched Melody, and I quietly giggled.

'It's so gross!' said Violet, and I could hear her whimpering.

I clicked open the door. They were all standing there covered from head to toe in thick green slime.

'Oh no, what happened?' I said with fake concern.

'It came from the ceiling,' wailed Melody.

But the ceiling was completely normal.

'I smell so bad,' said Kirsten, sniffing her shirt.

'You're right about that,' I said, clasping my nose.

'You better not tell anyone about this,' Violet snivelled, wiping the slime from her face.

'Oh, I won't,' I replied and seized my sketchbook from her.

I wiped it clean with a paper towel as Kirsten went into the cubicle I'd been in.

'Did you draw this?' she said, looking at my drawing on the wall.

I gave a half-hearted shrug.

Violet and Melody went to take a look.

'Is that supposed to be us?' said Violet. 'But how could that be? You've got us covered in green gunk just like what we're covered in now.'

'Did you know this was going to happen to us?' said Melody.

I crossed my arms, my head tilted to the side. 'Maybe I'm a witch who's put a terrible spell on you,' I snarled, stepping towards them. I made my eyes look wild for extra scare and the Vile-lets did look scared stiff.

'Keep bothering me or Doug and I'll put another spell on you – one that'll be ten times more disgusting,' I warned as all three of them gulped in unison.

'Just stay away from us,' said Violet, squirming back from me.

'Only if *you* stay away from me and Doug.'

'We don't want to be anywhere near you!' Violet bawled.

'Good,' I replied. And with that, I left the toilets.

'Freak!' Kirsten called out after me.

But for once their words didn't hurt. And for the first time, I didn't feel the slightest bit afraid.

CHAPTER 32

The next day I was in BIG trouble! When the bell went for morning break, Mrs Downing asked me to stay back, and straight away I was worried because she had a very serious look on her face.

'Mr Nelson would like to see you in his office, Prune,' she said to me. 'It's about an incident that took place in the girls toilets yesterday.'

I gulped and began to feel really guilty, not just because of the slime that I'd brought to life, but because I'd broken my own promise not to use my superpower again. And my guilt only intensified when I arrived at Mr Nelson's office to find Mama already sitting there.

'Prune,' said Mama when Mr Nelson had stepped out of the room to get her a glass of water, 'I'd only just arrived at work when I got a call from Mr Nelson requesting to see me.' She looked so disappointed. 'It's bad enough I have your brother's school calling me, but now I've got yours too! So what have you been up to, Prune? Why am I here?'

But before I could answer her, Mama looked up at the ceiling and said, 'Lord, please don't let me have another child that's skipping school.'

'I haven't been,' I said, 'and I don't know why you're here.'

'Well, whatever the reason, I know it's not for anything good. Looks like you're in a lot of trouble, young lady.'

Mr Nelson returned with the glass of water for Mama.

'Thank you for coming here at such short notice,' he said to her. 'I expect you're wondering why I wanted to speak to you in person.'

'I am indeed,' said Mama, sitting completely straight like she was in trouble herself.

'Well, I'm sorry to tell you this, but Prune has done something very reckless,' said Mr Nelson.

I swallowed nervously.

'What has she done?' asked Mama, shooting me a look that could kill a creature stone dead.

'She's damaged school property,' said Mr Nelson.

Mama looked at him like he was making no sense.

'She drew some graffiti in the girls toilets,' he clarified.

So the Vile-lets had gone and snitched on me. Though I'd hardly call my drawing graffiti!

'*Graffiti*,' said Mama. 'But Prune's a good girl. She wouldn't do something like that.'

'Although the incident was reported to us by other pupils, some pictures were also found in the toilets that had the same style of drawing as the graffiti. Prune's teacher, Mrs Downing, was able to identify both the graffiti and the pictures as being *Prune's handiwork*,' said Mr Nelson, raising his brows as he said this. 'At Maple Lane, we have a zero-tolerance rule when it comes to behaviour of this kind. I hope you understand that, Prune.'

'Oh, she most definitely does,' Mama answered for me, but Mr Nelson still looked at me for a reaction.

I nodded.

'What you did was unacceptable.'

'Sorry, Mr Nelson,' I mumbled.

He turned to Mama again. 'In normal circumstances, Prune would be excluded for a short period, but as she's still fairly new, I'm willing to let it slide on this occasion,' he said as I hung my head.

Mama nudged me to look back up.

'But this is going to be your last warning,' said Mr

Nelson. 'If you attempt to do any graffiti again or anything else that contravenes school policy, then I'm afraid I will have to exclude you.'

'Oh, she won't do anything like that again – you have my word on that,' said Mama earnestly. Then throwing me another angry look, she mouthed, *'How could you shame me like this?'* and my heart plummeted.

'I also wanted to ask you, Prune, if you knew anything about a green substance that was found in the toilets?' said Mr Nelson.

I gulped and quickly shook my head.

'I don't believe you're responsible, but I thought I'd ask. It's more than likely a plumbing issue, though Mr Welch, our caretaker, has yet to work out exactly where it came from. Unfortunately, it fell on to a few pupils, who got completely soaked.'

Of course, Mama didn't know he was referring to the Vile-lets.

'Do you know anything about this, Prune?' she asked.

I shook my head again. 'No, Mama, I don't – honest.'

'Right,' said Mr Nelson, 'I think it would be best for Prune to end her school day now, give her a chance to think about what she's done. But I look forward to seeing her back at school tomorrow.'

'I'm so sorry for my daughter's behaviour, Mr Nelson,

and I swear to you that it'll never happen again,' said Mama, hauling me up and scowling at me as we left his office.

I braced myself for an earful, expecting Mama to do it right in front of the school secretary. She didn't, and neither did she in the car on our way home. Instead, she waited until we were in the house with all the windows closed before she let rip.

'Why, why, why did you do that, Prune?' she thundered. 'Why would you go and damage school property?'

'I didn't mean to.'

'So why on earth did you do it?'

Tears filled my eyes.

'There are these girls, Mama, and ever since I started the school, they've done nothing but pick on me.'

'Does your teacher know about this? Does Mr Nelson?'

I shook my head.

'In that case, I'm going to go back up to that school and make sure they put a stop to it,' she said, her arms folded. 'I'll show that head teacher of yours what "zero tolerance" really means, because no *way* is anyone going to bully my child!'

'I found a way to make them stop. Or, I thought I had,' I replied.

'But that still doesn't explain why you put up that graffiti. And what kind of graffiti was it?' said Mama.

'It was a drawing of them covered in slime.'

'Well, that certainly sounds imaginative, I'll give you that,' she replied, her face softening a little.

'But that's not all …' I swallowed. 'I made the drawing come to life. I made them get covered in real slime.'

'You did *what*?' said Mama, her face becoming cross again. 'I distinctly told you that you weren't to use your power. I just knew it would lead to trouble – or something we couldn't explain.'

'But they destroyed my pictures, Mama! They deserved it.'

'I understand how you feel, Prune, and those girls sound like they've been extremely cruel, but you can't just go around misusing your power like that,' said Mama.

'It was only slime.'

'Yes, but it could've injured them.'

Mama went and sat on the sofa and patted the seat next to her for me to sit down as well.

'What if one of the teachers had found out about your ability?' she said, her hand on top of mine. 'We can't afford for people to find out about this, Prune – not when we don't know what the consequences might be and what it could mean for our family. For all we know, social services could turn up here asking all sorts of questions, and who's to say they won't want to separate us.'

My lip quivered. 'I'm sorry, Mama.'

I'd never want to be separated from her and Jesse.

'I don't mean to scare you, Prune, but keeping you and your brother safe is all that matters to me. That's why you can't use your power. Do you understand?'

I nodded but then fled up to my room, where I burst into tears.

A short while later, Mama knocked on my door, full of apology.

'I'm sorry for upsetting you, Prune,' she whispered, sitting down on the edge of my bed. But I kept my back to her, my head buried in my pillow. 'I just wanted you to know how serious it was, you using your power to get revenge on those girls.' She drew in a breath. 'You know, I wondered to myself the other day what your dad would make of this superpower of yours if he was still in our lives. Though I do know that whatever he might think, he'd still love you just the same – just like I do and always will.'

'He was here,' I murmured.

'Huh?'

I turned over to face her. 'I thought I could bring him back. But I was just being stupid.'

Mama looked at me, confused.

'I drew a picture of him and made him come alive,' I told her. 'Only the person wasn't Dad. He didn't have any of his memories and he didn't behave like Dad at all. He was a complete fake! But I only brought him to life because I wanted to see him and let him know that I missed him.'

'Oh, Prune,' said Mama, pulling me in for a cuddle as my tears returned. 'It's all right, sweetheart – I know you miss your dad.'

She pulled back and looked at me for a minute then sighed. 'I think it's time we told Jesse about your super-power.'

'Really?' I looked at Mama with surprise.

She nodded. 'I don't think it's fair to continue keeping him in the dark when he's as much a part of this family as you and I. And if anything were to happen, not that I'm saying it will, then we need to be able to be there for each other.'

'But I'm not sure he's going to believe me unless I show him. I tried telling him when he saw Alf, but he thought I was making it all up! So I might have to use my power, Mama.'

'Yeah, he probably will want to see it.' She nodded again. 'OK, you can show him when he gets in.'

CHAPTER 33

When Jesse got home, he looked convinced Mama was about to give him a telling-off.

'I've not been bunking off school, Mama, if that's what you're thinking,' he said as Mama looked at him with a grave face, the three of us all sitting around the kitchen table.

'What I'm about to tell you, Jesse, has nothing to do with you and school,' said Mama.

'So what's it about, and how comes you're home early?'

'There was an incident at Prune's school, but it's all sorted now,' she said. 'But there is something else you need to know about your sister.'

'What is it?' said Jesse, his face suddenly clouding with worry.

'It's nothing for you to be scared about but …' She hesitated for a second. 'Your sister has an ability.'

Jesse's eyes flitted back and forth between the both of us. 'An *ability*,' he repeated. 'Like what? An ability to get on my nerves!' He smirked.

'I can bring my pictures to life,' I piped up. 'I have a superpower.'

For a brief moment, Jesse looked perplexed before throwing his head back with laughter. 'Oh, not this *again*! And I can't believe, Prune, you've got Mama involved. Well, I have to say, this little game you've got going is hilarious.'

'It's not a game, Jesse,' said Mama sharply.

'Yeah, it's not!' I said. 'I drew Alf and brought him to life – I tried telling you! – and I even brought to life a zoo.'

'Look, I don't know if anyone has told you this, Prune,' said Jesse in a condescending voice, 'but in real life, people don't have superpowers. I think you've been watching far too many films. In fact, only in your dreams, Prune, would you ever be able to bring your pictures to life—'

'She *does* have a superpower,' said Mama, about to lose her patience.

'No – I'm not buying any of this,' said Jesse. 'And I don't have time for it either.'

He stood up.

'Sit back down,' said Mama, her eyes firmly fixed on him.

He did so with a sigh and turned to me. 'Look, Prune, if you really want to convince me you have a superpower, then I'm going to have to see it for myself,' said Jesse, just as I expected him to say.

I stood up. 'OK, I'll show you.'

'This is going to be *so* fun. Not,' he jibed.

I rolled my eyes then went to fetch my sketchbook and pencils.

'So what would you like me to bring to life?' I asked Jesse once I'd returned.

My brother laughed again. 'All right, I'm going to go along with this charade, but honestly, Prune, this has to be the dumbest game ever.'

He put his hand to his chin and pretended to think seriously about what he wanted me to draw. 'Mama, what's for dinner?'

'I was planning on making us some spaghetti bolognese,' she told him.

'Nah, I want pizza. Prune, draw me a pepperoni pizza with lots of cheese and peppers, and while you're at it, draw me a hamburger.'

'OK, one pizza and hamburger coming up,' I said and started to draw.

'And how long is this drawing going to take?' said Jesse after a couple of minutes.

'I'm trying to be as quick as I can,' I replied. 'Do you want lettuce in your hamburger?'

'Yeah, I'll have some lettuce.'

After a few more minutes, I was done.

Jesse inspected my picture. 'Well, one thing I'll say is that this drawing looks almost real enough to eat. Good job, sis, but I think I'll go and get myself some real food from the cupboard,' he scoffed and got up from the table again.

'Just wait –' Mama put a hand out to stop him – 'and watch.'

Sitting back down, Jesse pretended to yawn, but I stayed focused on summoning the colours.

Jesse was about to eat his words.

'Whoa ...' was all my brother could say as the pizza and hamburger appeared on the table, his face completely awestruck.

And I said, '*Now* do you believe me?'

'Um ...' he muttered, looking at the platter of food cautiously.

'So are you going to try it or are you just going to stare at it?' asked Mama.

'Er, OK,' he mumbled, then very slowly Jesse picked up a slice of pizza.

His face creased with uncertainty as his tongue touched the very tip of it like he was trying to check that it really was pizza. He took a small bite and chewed thoughtfully.

'It tastes good,' he hummed.

He ate some more until he'd finished the whole slice ... then he ate another slice, and then another. Next, he took a large bite out of the hamburger.

He grinned. 'This is good too,' he said and gobbled the rest of it down before polishing off the remaining slices of pizza.

Mama shook her head. 'You'll make yourself sick, eating like that.'

'I've got to hand it to you, sis – that burger was the real deal,' Jesse exclaimed. 'In fact, it was the best hamburger I've ever tasted, seriously. And your pizza was way better than any of the pizzas Big Sal's does. So, I admit, for a minute you almost had me fooled.'

Then he burst out laughing again.

'Don't think I didn't know you were hiding the burger and pizza under the table the whole time. Honestly, sis, you're going to have to do a lot better than that if you want to convince me you have a superpower. No doubt you learned that trick off YouTube and used something like invisible ink to make the picture disappear from your sketchbook.'

'No, Jesse,' said Mama. 'It wasn't a magic trick. What you saw was real.' She looked him square in the eye. 'Why can't you just believe her?'

'Because there's no such thing as superpowers,' said Jesse, hunching his shoulders. He looked at me with his head to one side. 'But it's clear you want to carry on this sad little game. So, OK, you're saying you can bring *anything* to life – is that right?'

'Yes,' I said, exasperated.

'Even people?'

'Um, no,' I quickly fibbed. I didn't have the heart to tell my brother about my Fake Dad episode, plus Mama said nothing, so I guess she didn't mind me lying either.

'OK, if you can't draw people, then why don't you draw us a pet snake? No, a tiger?'

'A *tiger*? Jesse, are you out of your mind?' said Mama. 'I don't want some dangerous animal rampaging through my house – and since when has a tiger ever been a pet?'

'But how else does she expect me to believe her? It's not like a tiger is something you can hide under the table,' said Jesse and did a quick check as if to make sure.

I rolled my eyes in annoyance as I made a start on another picture.

'And what is it that you're drawing now?' said Jesse, trying to look, but I shielded my picture with my arm.

'You'll see,' I said simply. When I was done, I gently tore the picture out of my sketchbook and told Jesse, 'To see this, you'll need to come outside.'

'And why's that?' he asked, but I just smiled as I clutched my picture to my chest.

As we went out to the garden, I placed the picture at my feet. The afternoon sun was high in the sky and the clouds were all puffy and white.

Looking at my picture, Jesse started to laugh. 'Oh, don't tell me you're going to try and make it rain. Look, Prune, I seriously think you need to see a doctor, because you seem to be going a little bit cuckoo.'

'Hush, Jesse,' Mama snapped. 'Just let Prune do what she's got to do.'

'Uh, but this is so dumb,' he moaned.

'You won't be saying that when it does rain,' I replied before summoning the colours and silently commanding the picture to come to life. And as the drawing was swept up into the multicoloured funnel, suddenly a big grey cloud appeared above us looking just how I'd drawn it.

'Well, it does actually look like it's going to rain,' said Jesse. 'But don't go thinking I believe it's you doing this, Prune.'

A trickle of rain began to fall, and within seconds it was pelting down.

'Aaargh!! I'm getting soaked,' Jesse spluttered, pulling his school jumper over his head as he sprinted back into the house.

'Now do you believe her?' said Mama after I'd made the rain stop and the three of us had gone back inside.

'No,' Jesse rebuffed, wiping his wet face with some kitchen roll.

'Aw, *seriously*,' groaned Mama, and we both exchanged a look of frustration.

She left the kitchen and went upstairs to dry off.

'You're such a dimwit, Jesse,' I said to him as he picked up Mama's phone from the kitchen counter.

'What?! How am I the dimwit when it's not me pretending they can bring their drawings to life?'

'But I *can!*' I retorted, crossing my arms.

'Look, Prune, for the last time, you can't! And certainly not according to Mama's weather app,' he said, holding up her phone. 'The forecast says rain.'

Mama came back down with a towel over her head and a towel for both me and my brother. I put mine over my shoulder, and Jesse wiped his jumper with his.

'I can't believe I'm going to say this,' said Mama. 'Prune, just draw the tiger, because it looks like that's the only way you're going to get your brother to believe you.'

'Ooh, I can't wait to see this,' said Jesse, rubbing his

hands in fake glee. 'No doubt you'll present me with some teddy tiger.'

I ignored him and sat back down at the kitchen table. In my sketchbook, I began to draw a picture of a tiger. Jesse went and got a can of Pepsi from the fridge then watched over my shoulder as I continued to draw.

'Not bad,' he remarked.

When I was done, the three of us went back outside.

'I really can't wait for your teddy to appear,' Jesse teased.

But I took no notice as I summoned the colours a third time, silently wishing for the tiger to be real. The colours swiftly spun above my sketchbook, absorbing my drawing before disappearing altogether …

I held my breath.

CHAPTER 34

I'd never seen a tiger more magnificent. It was sitting just a few feet away, and this time Jesse looked truly spooked.

'Am I … am I dreaming, Mama?' he whispered as he gazed at it. 'That's a t-t-t-iger.'

My brother looked both astounded and terrified.

'No, you're not dreaming. And yes, that most definitely is a tiger,' said Mama, her face looking equally terrified. 'Just don't make a sound.'

Even though I'd drawn the tiger, I felt more frightened than a gazelle that knows it's about to be eaten – especially as I'd forgotten to say in my mind that I wanted the tiger to be tame. Yet the tiger looked as relaxed as Grandma used to when she'd sit in the garden soaking up some rays with a tall glass of lemonade. So perhaps the tiger was friendly like my zoo animals.

I took a few tentative steps forward.

'Prune, what are you doing?' hissed Mama as the tiger promptly sprang to his feet and stared straight at us. 'Get back here!'

The tiger now sort of looked like Mama, going from calm to moody, which is how she gets when Jesse and I forget to do our chores. But unlike the tiger, Mama doesn't have a massive jaw that could rip us in two.

My chest tensed.

'Oh my lord,' whispered Mama, and I swear not one of us breathed.

Then suddenly the tiger pounced forward.

'Run!' screeched Jesse, and we dashed back inside as fast as we could, slamming shut the door to the garden just as the tiger leaped against it.

'Make it disappear, Prune. Now!' Mama demanded.

I looked at the tiger as it stood up high against the door, pounding the glass with its paws.

I tried to get my mind to concentrate, but I was so scared, I couldn't get the tiger to vanish!

'Hurry up, Prune!' said Mama.

'I'm trying to!' I cried.

Disappear, disappear, disappear, I said over and over in my head while the tiger roared ferociously.

'It's going to get us!' shrieked Jesse.

I squeezed my eyes shut as I tried to concentrate again, imagining the tiger gone. Immediately the roaring stopped. The tiger had disappeared. I looked at my sketchbook and the tiger was back on the page, but instead of sitting down as I'd drawn him, he was standing on his hind legs with his jaws wide open.

'I don't think I've ever been so scared,' said Mama, her hand on her chest. 'But now do you believe your sister, Jesse?'

'Oh, I believe you,' he said, looking truly dumb-struck.

'*Finally*,' both Mama and I said with relief.

CHAPTER 35

'But how did you … ? When … ? Where did you get this from?' said Jesse, struggling to even speak.

He still couldn't quite get his head around the fact that I had a superpower.

'I don't know where I got it from,' I answered. 'But it's my power that makes me see the colours, and it's the colours that bring my drawings to life.'

'Interesting,' said Jesse. He peered at my drawing of the tiger. 'So when you made the tiger vanish, you basically trapped it back inside the picture.'

I nodded. 'But as you can see, the picture's changed.'

'To the tiger's last moment of being real,' said Jesse, sounding like he understood. '*Wow*,' he muttered.

'Well, I'm just pleased you believe her,' said Mama,

wandering out of the kitchen.

'But what I don't get is why I'm still hungry,' said my brother, rubbing his stomach. 'I mean, I ate a whole pizza and a hamburger.'

'Maybe it's because it wasn't *real* real food,' I said. 'After all, it did come out of a picture,' I added a little gloomily as an image of Fake Dad entered my head again.

'All of this just ... blows my mind,' said Jesse, shaking his head in bewilderment. 'My little sister has a superpower. It's *crazy* but at the same time pretty awesome.'

'And it means I could become a superhero and go to people's rescue. I could save their cats if they got stuck up a tree by bringing to life a ladder – or rescue people out of a burning building by bringing a trampoline to life so they could jump down on to it.'

'Yeah, you could, though I don't think Mama would want you going anywhere near a burning building. But I think you really can give yourself a superhero name now. So, what's it going to be?'

I shrugged. 'I don't know.'

'Well, if I had a superpower, I'd be the Invincible Jesse! ... Hang on, what if I do actually have a super-power but just don't know it yet? What if it's all genetic?'

'What might be genetic?' said Mama, coming back into the kitchen.

'Prune's superpower. If it is, then maybe I've got a superpower too but I just don't know it yet,' said Jesse.

'Sweet heavens! I don't think I could handle two kids with superpowers.' Mama visibly baulked at the idea. 'Though I'm afraid to say, Jesse, I don't think it is genetic – we simply don't know how Prune got hers.'

'Maybe she has a gene mutation sort of like the X-Men,' said Jesse. 'Or maybe, Prune, you're not even human.'

'I am human! But I'm a *super*human,' I corrected him.

'All right, but maybe something else gave you your superpower,' said Jesse.

I looked at him expectantly. 'Like what?'

'Like Delmere. You know how you were telling me about that Delmere Magic thing?'

I nodded.

'At first, I didn't really know what you were on about, but then I remembered that Poppa B did tell us about it,' Jesse started to explain. 'But he said it wasn't a story – it was all true. There really were kids with super-powers that killed some evil creature in ancient times.'

'Theo said their powers went into the ground,' I said, 'and that's how other kids developed superpowers—'

'That's all just silly folklore,' Mama jumped in with a cynical look on her face.

'Do you know about it, Mama?' I asked.

'Yes, because your grandfather told me the same

story when I was a kid. But I can assure you, sweetheart, none of it is true. Don't forget I grew up in Delmere, and to this day, except for you, I've never met *anyone* with a superpower.'

'But if it *is* true, then it might explain why Prune does have a power,' said Jesse. He stroked his chin for a second. 'We should go to the library and find out for ourselves.'

'I'm not sure how much you'll find about this Delmere Magic,' said Mama, 'but I think the both of you going to the library is a great idea.'

'Y'know, sis, you could actually rule the world if you wanted to!' said Jesse.

'So you're hoping your sister will become a ruthless dictator, are you?' said Mama, raising an eyebrow.

'No, I didn't mean it like that. What I meant was having a superpower means you can pretty much do anything, get anything. And I know just where Prune can start.'

A smile crept across Jesse's face. 'I'd love a moped!'

'Prune's ability isn't there for you to be turning her into your personal shopper, Jesse,' said Mama.

'Why not?' he said. 'You don't mind, do you, Prune?'

I was about to tell him that I actually didn't, but Mama interrupted.

'In life, things don't come for free, Jesse. If you want something, you work for it. That's why I'm always telling you how important it is to get a good education, so you can one day get a job that'll give you the money to buy all the things you want. And anyway, you're not old enough yet to ride a moped.'

'But you will let me use my superpower again, won't you?' I said, looking at Mama with pleading eyes.

She smiled gently. 'Look, I know I might not have been keen at first with you using your power, but I have had a bit of a think,' she said. 'As long as you promise to be responsible – and to make sure no one realises you have this power – then I don't mind you using it now and again … for the *right* reasons.'

'You really mean that?'

She nodded.

'Please don't be cross, Mama, but I told Corinne about my superpower – but she's promised not to tell anyone,' I said quickly.

Although Mama looked surprised, she wasn't cross. 'Well, I can understand you wanting to tell her. She is your best friend after all,' she replied. 'But when it comes to bringing stuff to life, I don't want you getting me a new car, and I definitely don't want you bringing to life another tiger, OK?'

'But can Prune still bring to life a moped?' my brother asked inquisitively.

'*No,*' said Mama. 'If you want a moped, Jesse, you

can go and get a weekend job and start saving up for one. And another thing – despite Corinne knowing about this, it's important we make sure nobody else finds out about your sister's ability. We can't be sure how people might react.'

'So you're going to have to keep it a secret, Jesse,' I told him, even though for me, keeping my power a secret was becoming harder by the day.

CHAPTER 36

I stuck to my word, and on Thursday morning I told Mrs Downing about the Vile-lets bullying me and Doug, about all the mean things they'd done and how they'd cornered me in the toilets and destroyed my pictures.

'So the drawings I found were what they'd ripped out of your sketchbook?' said Mrs Downing.

I nodded my head ruefully.

'Well, I'm so sorry that you and Doug have had to put up with what sounds like appalling behaviour.' Mrs Downing shook her head. 'And I'm sorry, Prune, I wasn't here so you could've told me sooner. It takes a lot of courage to come forward, and I understand it's not an easy thing to do, but I want you to know I'm always here to listen if you have any concerns at all.' She gave me a reassuring smile. 'This will be dealt with – I can promise you that. We take bullying very seriously at this school, so I'll be speaking to all three girls and will let Mr Nelson know about this too.'

It was such a relief to hear her say that. And sure enough, just before morning break, Mrs Downing asked the Vile-lets to stay behind while the rest of us went out and played. They looked mega worried as if they already knew they were in trouble. And later on, they were dead quiet as our class was eating lunch, and when Mr Nelson came up to our table, they looked terrified. He didn't say anything, but Violet, Melody and Kirsten immediately got up and followed him silently.

'I'm so pleased you told Mrs Downing,' whispered Doug through a mouthful of mashed potato. 'I hope this means they'll finally stop picking on us.'

'I think Mrs Downing will be keeping an eye on them from now on,' I said, 'so we shouldn't have to worry so much any more.'

'Surely there must be something else you'd like me to bring to life?' I said to Jesse when we both got in from school on Friday and plonked ourselves down on the living room sofa.

Jesse still wanted me to conjure up a moped, despite knowing it would be going against Mama's wishes if I did.

213

'I won't ride the moped – I just want to see it,' he kept saying.

'For the last time, Jesse, I'm not going to bring to life a moped, so will you stop asking me?' I told him in a firm voice. 'You heard Mama when she said I have to be responsible with my power.'

I really didn't want to get into Mama's bad books again, so creating a moped was simply out of the question.

Jesse sighed. 'All right, I'll stop going on. But I might ask you again when I'm old enough to ride one, just to warn you,' he said with a grin. 'However, there is something else you could bring to life that would be even better than a moped.'

'What?'

'A whale.'

I looked at Jesse with bemusement. 'Are you serious? A whale? As in a whale that lives in water? A whale that is a massive creature? That's what you want me to bring to life?'

Jesse's grin got bigger and I scrunched my face at him scathingly.

'You can be a right numbskull sometimes, Jesse. I mean, is it really too much for you to ask for something simple like a pair of jeans?'

'But that would be boring,' he responded. 'I thought you said you could just about make anything come to life.'

'I can.'

'So why not a whale?'

'Because, duh, look around you. Does this look like an ocean?'

'So why not just bring to life an ocean then?' Jesse replied blithely. 'Yeah, that would be epic if you could do that. We could go scuba diving!'

'But I don't know how that would work,' I murmured as a feeling of both excitement and trepidation stirred within me. 'What if I brought to life an ocean, and everybody and everything on this street and in this town ended up at the bottom of it?'

'I doubt that'll happen,' said Jesse.

'How do you know it won't? I'm the one with the superpower and I don't even know. I've never brought something that spectacular to life before.'

'Well, think about it scientifically,' said Jesse. 'Whatever you draw, it's on to paper first, right? So it's like the blank page is our reality, and your drawing is the layers on top of it.' He was getting animated now. 'Think of it like how rocks are formed with different strata. Our whole planet is made up of layers, so maybe the whole universe and your superpower are too.'

I threw my brother a bewildered look. He was making absolutely no sense whatsoever.

Jesse must have realised he'd confused me because

he then said, 'OK, don't think about rocks. Imagine a sandwich with the bottom slice being our house while the top slice is the ocean. But that top slice can't make the bottom slice all soggy because you've got a protective barrier in between made up of cheese or ham and lettuce.'

'What on earth have soggy sandwiches got to do with the ocean?' I questioned.

'No, the point is the sandwich wouldn't be soggy. Just take a moment to think about it?'

But thinking about sandwiches only made my tummy rumble.

'I've thought about it and I still don't get it,' I answered after a few seconds.

'OK, then think of it like a ... painting,' said Jesse. 'You, being the amazing artist you are, should know that paintings often have layers to them. So basically the ocean would be the top layer, while the layer underneath would be our house and Delmere. But they're two layers that never quite meet.'

I considered this then started to nod my head. I think I was beginning to understand, but I still couldn't help feeling apprehensive.

'But what if something was to go wrong? What if we find ourselves in the ocean but can't get back home?' I replied hesitantly.

As much as I was confident now in making things I'd brought to life disappear, what if there was a chance I couldn't make a whole ocean vanish?

'Don't worry, nothing will go wrong with me around,' said my brother, and I rolled my eyes.

But I decided to have a long think about this while Jesse went into the kitchen to make us both a sandwich.

If Jesse was wrong about this layer thing, and there *was* a chance our house could get flooded, then maybe there was a way I could make sure everything didn't get wet by just wishing for that not to happen. I'd brought to life the water in Alf's bowl, and while that was wet, it was contained. The difference this time was that the water would be on a bigger scale and our house would sort of be like Alf's bowl.

Once Jesse had finished making the sandwiches, I was ready to tell him my decision.

'OK, I'll draw an ocean,' I announced as I took a bite.

'Yes!' Jesse cheered, raising his arms in the air.

I put down my half-eaten sandwich and started on the picture, drawing lots of fish as well as coral, seaweed, sea horses and sea turtles – and then finally the whale. I don't know why, but I drew a blue whale, which happens to be the largest mammal on the planet.

What was I thinking?

Although I'd heard blue whales don't pose a threat to humans, I decided to make sure the whale was tame, just to be on the safe side. On another page, I drew a pair of diving wetsuits and breathing equipment, which of course we were going to need.

'Your drawings look terrific, Prune,' said Jesse after I'd finished.

'I am still a little worried about bringing it all to life,' I admitted.

'Don't be. Just think of it as homework – we're going to be learning about the ocean by actually being in one,' said Jesse.

I nodded, clearing any doubts from my mind, then stood up with my pictures.

'Right then, here goes,' I said and summoned the colours.

First I brought to life the wetsuits and breathing equipment.

'Wow, it's a real air tank and a real wetsuit,' said Jesse, completely amazed again as he inspected it all.

We got changed into the wetsuits then hooked up our air tanks and put on our diving masks. And when Jesse was ready, he gave me a thumbs up.

I desperately didn't want anything to go wrong, and as we stood in the middle of the living room, I took a moment to compose myself before summoning the colours once again. And as they blossomed around me and Jesse, I made my wish for the ocean to be real, for our house to stay safe and dry, and for the whale to be tame.

The colours started to spin and so did the room as it immediately began to fall away around us, the furniture vanishing into thin air, and the walls tumbling down. Instinctively I felt scared.

What was happening?!

Then suddenly there was water at our feet. Jesse's eyes widened in alarm as he grabbed my hand, the water rapidly getting higher and higher until it had reached my knees, then my waist, then my shoulders, and then Jesse was no longer holding my hand!

SPLASH!! I found myself sinking down, down, down until I was deep inside the ocean. I quickly tried to find my brother, who thankfully was close by. His eyes were still wide but this time in wonderment.

My ocean was truly astonishing and more beautiful than any ocean I'd seen in a geography book or on the telly. And everything I'd drawn was there – the coral, the seaweed, the sea turtles and the numerous fish that we swam amongst.

Then my whale came into view.

Both Jesse and I froze as we watched the whale swim past, and the whole thing almost felt never-ending because the creature was so huge, while I felt as tiny as a pea. My heart was beating really fast, but I don't think the whale even noticed us nor did she seem bothered when Jesse went up to stroke her. I was completely blown away, my beating heart becoming full of joy at what I was seeing. With the ocean feeling so real and so huge, it certainly didn't feel like we were still in our living room. And there was a part of me that wanted to stay in this amazing underwater world forever.

As the whale swam away, Jesse and I continued to explore the ocean, looking at the coral and watching the sea turtles swim about. All of a sudden I could hear music. But then I realised it was actually a phone ringtone – Jesse's phone to be exact. So we really hadn't left our house at all.

Although his phone had stopped ringing, I pointed upwards to indicate to Jesse we should return. He nodded and I took one last moment to admire the ocean. Then I slowly imagined it all disappearing, and very quickly the walls of our living room started to lift back up. The mantelpiece reappeared, followed by the sofa, the TV, the coffee table and the rest of our furniture, all exactly as they were and in the same place. We were back, with the only reminder of our ocean adventure being the tiny puddle of water at our feet.

I had done it!

'That was phenomenal!' said Jesse, taking off his diving mask. He gave me a hug. 'To think we used to live in a place called Ocean View but only today did we get to view a real ocean, *our ocean*, Prune, and I'm never going to forget a single minute of it.'

'Me neither,' I replied.

'And the fact you were able to create an ocean, Prune – just imagine what other unbelievable things you could bring to life. You could create your own version of an Egyptian pyramid or even planet Mars, or you could bring to life your own tropical island.'

'Yeah, I really could, couldn't I?' I smiled.

Jesse's phone started ringing again, and as he collected it from the coffee table, the look of joy on his face seemed to disappear faster than our ocean had.

'Yeah, no problem – I can do that,' he said to the caller before hanging up.

'Don't tell me. That was Bryce, wasn't it?' I said.

For a second I thought Jesse would deny this, but he replied, 'Yeah, it was.'

I frowned. 'And what did *he* want? And what were you telling him you can do?'

'He'd forgotten the title of a new video game I'd told him about. He wants me to text it to him.'

'Oh, does he now?' I replied, cynically.

'He does, Prune, but I'd rather not get into an

argument about Bryce if that's OK – not when I've just had the most unforgettable experience ever,' said Jesse. 'I still can't believe I stroked an actual blue whale,' he added, a look of joy returning to his face. 'Today has been one of the best days of my life.'

It had been one of the best days of my life as well – a day that I would always cherish. A day that not even Bryce could spoil.

CHAPTER 37

On Saturday morning Jesse and I went to the library on the high street to see if we could find anything about the Delmere Magic.

'So where do you want to start?' he said as we went inside.

'I'm not sure,' I answered as I surveyed the shelves of books in front of us.

'We can go and ask if they have an archive or something,' said Jesse.

So we spoke to a librarian and told her that we were doing some research into the history of Delmere. She suggested a few books, which she fetched for us, and showed us their online newspaper archive.

So while I sat at a computer searching through

articles, Jesse looked through the books. At first, I couldn't find any articles on people who might've had superpowers. Most of the clippings seemed to be about sports or politics. But then, after doing some more searching, I came across a peculiar article from 15th June 1954.

CHILD 'BRINGS BABY BROTHER BACK TO LIFE' read the headline. It was about a nine-year-old girl called Beatrice Clarke whose parents believed she had healing powers and had brought her eighteen-month-old brother, Edmund, back to life. His death had been confirmed by a doctor. However, the next day the baby was discovered by his parents alive and well, playing happily in his cot with Beatrice by his side.

And there was this other old article – *FROZEN CAT MYSTERY DEEPENS* – which was about a cat that was found completely frozen right here on the high street back in the 1980s on what was the hottest day of the year. And this was the interesting thing – an elderly lady called Hilda Jennings said she saw a small boy stroking the cat moments before it was found frozen solid in a block of ice.

I showed Jesse the articles.

'I think these kids had superpowers, Jesse,' I whispered. 'The girl was able to bring her brother back to life, and it looks like there was a little boy who could freeze things.'

'Blimey, that's certainly something,' he said. 'And you'll never guess what I found.'

He showed me a page from one of the books he'd been looking at.

'It's all about the Delmere Magic. The kids were from a prehistoric tribe. They called the creature the Vellibog – it lived under the ground, and every thirty-four years, to be exact, the creature would rise and eat the children's souls.'

I gasped. 'Which is exactly what Theo said!'

There was an artist's impression of what the creature looked like: a dark shadow with hollow eyes and a snarling mouth with razor-sharp teeth.

Jesse turned over to the next page. 'It says here when the creature was due to rise for the eighteenth time, the tribe's elders performed a spell to give the children the strength to fight it. Although the spell had failed in the past, this time it worked, and the children were gifted with tremendous powers.'

I quickly scanned the page. 'And just like Theo told me, when the kids destroyed the creature, the energy from their powers went into the ground,' I said. 'And that was the ground Delmere was built on.' I sighed as I glanced back at the computer screen. 'The problem with these articles, Jesse, is that they're really old – so there's no way of knowing if there are other kids right now who have a superpower.'

'Well, maybe like you, they're just keeping it a secret. So you never know, there might just be kids in this town who are super strong or can walk through walls.'

I smiled. 'Yeah, or maybe kids who can grow limbs, or stretch their bodies like elastic!'

'Or kids who can pause time or flash forward into the future!' said Jesse. 'And what do you reckon they would call a kid who could do that?'

I shrugged.

'Ed.'

'Huh?'

'As in *a-h-e-a-d* of time. You'd call him Ed for short.' He sighed. 'You don't get it, do you?'

'I do, but it's just not a very good joke,' I responded. 'I think you're losing your touch, Jesse.'

However, Jesse's face was deep in thought. 'Hey, let me see that article about the frozen cat again.'

'OK,' I said and clicked back on to the article.

Jesse looked at the screen. 'It's dated third August 1988. That was thirty-four years ago. And the article about the girl, Beatrice Clarke, was thirty-four years before that.'

I looked at Jesse quizzically. 'And … ?'

'Can't you see? There's a pattern here,' he replied. 'I have a theory. The Vellibog was returning every thirty-four years, but that all stopped after the kids' powers went into the ground. So maybe what's happening is that every thirty-four years, the ground gets kind of re-energised with their powers, and maybe that's what's giving some kids in Delmere superpowers.'

'That's actually not a bad theory,' I said, nodding. 'Y'know, you could make a great detective one day if you change your mind about becoming a professional basketball player.'

'Cheers, but I think I'll stick to basketball,' he said with a smile. 'Though one thing you need to keep in mind, Prune, is that there still could be another reason why you got your power, but I guess we may never truly know.'

Jesse put down the book he was holding. 'Anyway, all this research has got me parched. I'm going to go over to the shop and get a drink. Do you want one?'

'No, I'm OK.'

'Cool, I'll see you in a bit,' said Jesse.

But after a couple of minutes, I realised that I was feeling rather thirsty too. So I decided I'd go over to the shop myself. But when I left the library, I immediately froze, my mouth flipping open at the sight of Jesse talking to Bryce.

Then I saw Bryce pass something to Jesse through the window of his car, not that I could properly see what it was. Jesse slipped it into his rucksack, then they bumped fists and Bryce drove off.

I walked over to Jesse with my arms folded.

'What did Bryce want?'

'You don't need to know, Prune,' he said, and there was a tense look on Jesse's face.

'I saw him give you something. What was it?'

'I don't know what you're talking about. He didn't give me anything.'

'Don't lie.'

Jesse rolled his eyes.

'Look, if you must know, he gave me a can of 7up. He saved me that trip to the shop.' He pulled a can of drink out from his rucksack, but I noticed his hands were shaking.

'So he came all this way to give you a can of 7up? But how did he even know you were at the library?'

'He was just passing by and happened to spot me.'

'He seems to be passing by a lot, don't you think?' I said.

'Look, Prune, I know you don't like Bryce, but he's my best friend and he's always had my back, so will you just get off my case?!'

'Suit yourself,' I replied.

But as we walked back home I couldn't shake off the feeling that Bryce and Jesse had something planned, something I just knew was bad. I thought back to the night when Bryce came to the house and said how he was *counting on* Jesse. Then there was Bryce's phone call yesterday, which I didn't believe for one second was to find out the title of a video game.

Jesse was clearly in trouble. But how could I help him get out of it?

CHAPTER 38

'So what kind of things do they teach you at your computer club?' I asked Jesse while we were eating a cheese omelette for lunch, which Mama had made for us before popping out to the shops.

'It's coding stuff mostly,' he said. 'It's quite interesting.'

'So does this mean you're starting to like your school now?'

'Well, I suppose the place is beginning to grow on me, but I wouldn't say I completely like it just yet,' Jesse stated. 'What about you? Did those girls give you any bother yesterday?'

'No, they've been leaving me alone, so everything at school is all good now.'

I'd already told Jesse and Mama how I'd reported the

Vile-lets to Mrs Downing, but I'd given Jesse a further update. According to Mrs Downing, Melody admitted to Mr Nelson that she, Violet and Kirsten had been picking on me and Doug, and Mr Nelson was planning to speak to their parents.

'So are you looking forward to your sleepover tonight?' asked Jesse.

I'd arranged another sleepover with Corinne, at her house this time.

'Yeah, I can't wait,' I replied.

'And are you planning on bringing anything to life?'

'I might if Corinne wants me to.'

'And speaking of things being brought to life, I was wondering if there was something else you could make real.'

'Oh, it's not a lion you're wanting this time, is it? Or something even more extreme like a dinosaur?'

'Well, you're spot on because I've always wanted to meet a *Tyrannosaurus rex*,' said Jesse. Then he started chuckling. 'Don't worry, I'm joking. What I'm looking for isn't as dramatic as that. I was just going to ask if you could bring to life a basketball hoop in the garden, and perhaps we could shoot some hoops together.'

'Sure, I don't mind drawing that,' I said simply. 'Shooting some hoops would be fun,' I added and opened my sketchbook.

'I don't know why I didn't ask you before, as having a hoop will give me the chance to get in some regular practice, especially if I manage to get a try-out with my school's basketball team,' said Jesse.

'Well, it'll only take me a minute or two to draw this.'

'Cool, I'll go and get my ball,' said Jesse as he headed upstairs.

When I finished the drawing, I took my sketchbook outside, and once I'd summoned the colours and willed the picture to come to life, a shiny basketball hoop swiftly appeared in our garden. I waited for Jesse to return with his ball, but he was taking forever.

I went back into the house and called up to him from the bottom of the stairs. He didn't respond. I sighed and trundled up, going straight into his room. 'I thought you wanted to shoot some—?'

'What are you doing just barging in? Get out!' Jesse barked as I noticed him slip something under his bed sheet.

'What have you got there?'

'I told you, get out,' said Jesse, shooing me with his hand.

But curiosity had got the better of me. 'I want to know what you're hiding.'

I approached the bed.

'No!' he said, pushing me back towards the door.

232

'I want to see what it is.'

'And I want you out of my room!'

I swiftly loosened myself from his grip and scurried over to the bed, lifting the sheet before Jesse could stop me – and lying there was an iPhone.

I blinked at him. 'Where did you get this from?'

Jesse rolled his eyes. 'None of your business.'

'But this isn't your phone.' I looked across to Jesse's desk. 'That's your phone,' I said, pointing at the Nokia on top of it. 'So where did you get it, Jesse?'

'Jeez! You and your questions, Prune,' he grunted, snatching up the iPhone and slipping it into his trouser pocket. 'I wanted to get a new one, all right. A phone that would be way better than that tired old phone Mama gave me.'

I crossed my arms.

'I don't believe you, because it's not as if you've been saving up all of your pocket money to afford a phone like that. And why were you trying to hide it?'

'I wasn't …' Jesse paused then let out a sigh as he sat back down on his bed. 'OK, if you must know, I'm looking after it.'

'Looking after it?' I repeated, confused.

'Bryce gave it to me outside the library,' said Jesse slowly. 'He said he wanted me to keep hold of it for a while.'

'I knew it! I knew he hadn't given you a drink. So, whose phone is it? His?'

Jesse shrugged.

'The phone, it's not … stolen, is it?' I said as my heart began to thump.

'I dunno. It might be,' Jesse muttered.

'What?! Are you crazy, Jesse? If that phone's stolen, then you could get into serious trouble.'

'I said it *might be*, meaning there's a chance it hasn't been stolen.'

'I don't trust Bryce, and you shouldn't trust him either.'

'But, Prune – me and Bryce, we're like brothers, so I've got to trust him,' said Jesse, not that his face looked convinced by what he was saying.

'I bet you've not really been going to an after-school club,' I said, my head to one side. 'You made it up, didn't you? To cover the fact you've been hanging out with Bryce. I just knew you were both up to something.'

'I've not made it up. I really do go to an after-school club.'

Just then we heard the front door open and close.

'Kids, I'm back!' Mama trilled.

Jesse stepped out of the room. 'We're just upstairs, Mama,' he told her.

He then came back in.

'I wonder what Mama would say if she knew you had a stolen phone in our house?' I said.

'Please, Prune, you can't tell her. Promise me you won't,' said Jesse urgently.

A look of worry spread across his face.

'I will, but only if *you* promise to give the phone back to Bryce.'

'It's not that simple.'

'Why not?'

'Because Bryce says that if I don't keep quiet about it, then there's going to be problems. And I certainly know what he means when he says that.'

I did too, and I definitely didn't want my brother getting beaten up, but I also knew Bryce was a bully just like the Vile-lets.

'Weren't you the one who told me the best way to deal with a bully was to stand tall and show them you're not scared?' I said to Jesse.

'Yeah, I did say that, didn't I? Only, standing up to Bryce isn't going to be easy,' he mumbled.

'Well, you have to try, Jesse. You have to let him know that he can't keep pushing you around.'

'I wish I could feel that brave,' he muttered.

'The night Bryce came here, what did he mean when he said he was counting on you?' I asked, the memory of that night popping into my head again.

Jesse sighed. 'He came to tell me that he was planning to get hold of a few phones, which I guess included this one. So he was counting on me not to say anything to anyone.'

'So he's actually got a whole stash of stolen phones?!'

'Yeah.' Jesse nodded. 'I know I'm just kidding myself wanting to believe this phone hasn't been stolen. But I think Bryce is planning to sell it along with the other phones.'

'I know I've already asked you this, but were those trainers Bryce got for you stolen?' I said.

Jesse nodded again. 'But I wasn't with him the day he stole them, I swear.'

'That doesn't excuse the fact you've got a pair of stolen trainers!' I shook my head at him, the shock of it sinking in.

'I know, but I've only worn them a few times, and I have no intention of wearing them again.'

'But what will Bryce give to you next that's been stolen? Can't you see? Things are only going to get worse,' I said. 'That's why you need to stop being friends with Bryce before you end up in young offenders. And don't expect him to care if that happens – Bryce only cares about himself.'

'I'll make sure it doesn't come to that.'

'But it will if you keep hanging around with Bryce!'

'Kids, can you come and help me unpack the shopping?' Mama called.

Jesse went up to the door and opened it slightly. 'Sure, Mama, we'll be down in a sec!' he called back. 'We're just feeding Alf.'

He closed the door and turned back round.

'Truth is, Prune, I don't think I want to be friends with Bryce any more. And recently I've been trying to keep my distance – that's why I've been going to that computer club.'

His face sank into a huge frown.

'I wish I could give the phone back and the trainers, but I know Bryce won't let me do that without me facing some sort of punishment.'

Jesse has always been good at putting on a front, especially since our dad walked out on us, when he'd act like he wasn't bothered. But this was the first time I'd ever seen my brother look so afraid and seem so small despite the fact he's almost six feet tall.

'It's going to be all right,' I said as I tried to think of what I could do to help.

I gave him a hug, but I knew that wasn't going to be enough.

And it sure wasn't going to make the phone disappear.

CHAPTER 39

In the evening I went over to Corinne's for our sleepover. She still lives in the tower block we used to live in but on an even higher floor. Her flat is on the nineteenth floor on the other side of the building from our old flat. Corinne has much better views out of her windows than we used to get. She can see almost all of Ocean View and even catch a glimpse of the Shillbrook mountains in the faraway distance.

Unfortunately, when I arrived, Jesse and his phone were still playing on my mind and straight away Corinne could tell something was up.

So I told her everything and asked if she had any advice, because Corinne is really good at giving advice.

'So, do you think he should give the phone back?' I asked her, once I'd finished filling her in, as we sat cross-legged on her bed.

'Yes, I think he should, Prune, because if it is stolen, then he could get himself into huge trouble.' Corinne looked quite serious. 'So you should definitely speak to him again about it.'

I sighed. 'I think Jesse does realise now that Bryce is bad news. But yeah, I think I will speak to him again about giving the phone back. In fact, I'm going to insist that he does, and if he needs help when it comes to Bryce, then I could always use my superpower.'

'Yeah, you could bring to life a big dog to protect Jesse,' said Corinne.

'That's a good idea,' I replied.

'So how are you feeling about having to still keep your superpower a secret?' she asked.

I shrugged. 'I'm pleased that my mama doesn't mind me using my power, but I wish I *didn't* have to keep it a secret,' I said. 'Especially when there might be other kids like me.'

I told Corinne all about what Jesse and I had discovered at the library about the weird happenings in Delmere.

'If there really are other kids with superpowers, wouldn't it be cool if you got to meet them?' said

Corinne. 'And maybe you could all join forces and become like the Avengers.'

'Yeah, that would be *so* cool! Only, I still haven't decided what my superhero name would be.'

'What about the Supreme Artist?'

'Hmm, maybe,' I mused.

It felt like a really big decision.

Later on, after we'd eaten some of Corinne's snacks, I helped her go over some of her lines for *The Wizard of Oz.*

'Wouldn't it be amazing to be in the real Oz?' said Corinne at one point.

'Well, we could be!' I replied. 'I could just draw it and bring it to life.'

I'd already told Corinne all about how I'd brought to life an ocean along with a blue whale.

Her eyes twinkled. 'Awesome. I can't wait for this!'

I collected my sketchbook from my holdall and began to draw a picture of the yellow brick road and the Emerald City that I'd remembered from the film, while Corinne sat patiently until I'd finished.

'Right then – yellow brick road, here we come!' I said to Corinne as we both stood up and held each other's hands.

I summoned the colours then quietly willed the

picture to be real. Quickly, the colours spun above my sketchbook before sucking the picture out from the page. And just like when I created the ocean, the room began to spin and fall away, the walls being replaced with forest, and the floor turning into the yellow brick road. And within the blink of an eye, we were in Oz!

Corinne gasped. 'It's … wonderful,' she said, her eyes gazing at the stunning landscape.

Under our feet, the yellow brick road gleamed like a golden carpet, and in the faraway distance, the Emerald City looked even more dazzling than it did in the film. It sparkled like a billion jewels against what was the bluest sky I'd ever seen. And the luscious forest that surrounded us smelt of nothing that I'd smelt before. It was like the scent of all the trees and flowers you could think of.

'It's so pretty,' said Corinne, totally mesmerised. 'I love it, Prune!'

But then her eyes started to look a little worried. 'In the film, I'm sure the forest is supposed to be haunted.'

'Well, not this forest,' I said. 'So there's no need to worry. There won't be anything jumping out at us – no Wicked Witch or flying monkeys. It's just me and you here.'

There was nothing that felt unpleasant about the forest – in fact, it felt peaceful and safe.

Corinne and I skipped along the yellow brick road

arm in arm singing, 'We're off to see the wizard' before collapsing into a heap of giggles.

'So have we even left my bedroom?' said Corinne, as we lay flat on our backs gazing up at the sky.

'No, we're still in your room, but the yellow brick road is like a layer on top of it. Like the layers of a painting,' I said, repeating what Jesse had tried to explain to me. 'So what's underneath my brought-to-life picture is still there, if that makes sense?'

Corinne nodded and sat up. 'Kind of.' She smiled. 'Prune, could you bring something else to life?'

'Such as?'

'Um, I dunno. Surprise me.'

'OK, but I'll have to get my sketchbook, so we'll have to go back to your room.'

We took one last look at Oz before I imagined it all gone, and within seconds Corinne's bedroom started coming back into focus, the walls and ceiling returning, and the yellow brick road changing back into her laminate floor.

'Home sweet home,' said Corinne. 'But I will miss Oz.'

'We can always return there at our next sleepover,' I said, and we both shared a grin.

I got to work on my next picture and summoned the colours again. And as I brought the picture to life, Corinne's face beamed.

Above us, her ceiling had completely vanished and was replaced by stars. I'd recreated the night sky right in her bedroom. It was beautiful and it was like we were in outer space. The stars were so bright and low enough for us to pluck straight out of the sky.

'They look so real,' said Corinne, holding a star, her face glowing in its light.

'Well, I guess you can't fit a real star into your hands …'

'But it's probably the closest I'm ever going to get to one. Thank you, Prune, for doing all of this,' she said, hugging me.

With her music playing, Corinne and I spent the evening dancing around her bedroom with the stars shining down on us.

As we flopped down on the bed, we agreed it'd been our best sleepover yet. What could be better than getting to sleep under the stars with your best friend?

It was just a shame that the next day I would have to make it all disappear.

CHAPTER 40

Mama picked me up from Corinne's on Sunday, and when we got back home, the first thing I did was go and speak to Jesse.

'Can I come in?' I said, poking my head around his door.

He put down the comic he was reading and I went and sat on his bed.

'I really think you should give the phone back, because you're only going to cause more problems for yourself, Jesse.'

He sighed. 'I have been thinking it over. In fact, I've done nothing except think about that phone. Honestly, Prune, I'm scared of what might happen if I do give it back to Bryce. But I'm also scared of what could happen if I don't.'

'But giving the phone back to Bryce is a much better option than keeping hold of it,' I replied. 'You know I could come with you when you hand it back.'

Jesse shook his head. 'No, Prune, I can't let you.'

'But I'll protect you.'

He looked at me quizzically. 'I don't need a body-guard, Prune – and anyway, you're just a kid.'

'A kid who's got a superpower, don't forget, so I could draw something to keep us safe.'

'I'm sorry to tell you this, Prune, but drawing, say, a can of baked beans or another goldfish isn't going to do much if Bryce and the others decide they want to beat me up. And there's no way I want you getting hurt, so if I'm going to do this, I'm doing it alone.'

'Well, I'll draw a dog that's big and scary,' I said, remembering what Corinne had suggested.

But Jesse looked at me sceptically. 'Look, I don't need you drawing me anything, Prune. I can handle this by myself.'

'But what if you can't, Jesse? I mean, if Bryce does try to beat you up and I'm there, at least I can try and call for help. And I promise I'll stay in the background.'

He gave me a searching look. 'I've got to be mad to agree to this … Oh, all right, you can come. But I will need you to stay back, *way back*. We'll go to Ocean View tomorrow after school. I'll call Bryce, let him know I want us to meet.'

'Good,' I said, feeling rather relieved. I put my hand on his shoulder. 'It is going to be OK, Jesse.'

Giving me the tiniest of smiles, he replied, 'I hope so.'

As I left Jesse's room, my heart began to thud at the thought of going up against Bryce. But there was no way I was going to let him or anyone else hurt my brother. Jesse had always been there for me – now it was my turn to be there for him, which meant I'd have to be brave and strong, just like a superhero should be.

That night I struggled to get off to sleep, a panicky feeling stirring in the depths of my tummy at the thought of me and Jesse having to stand up to Bryce. Then suddenly a shaft of white light crept into my bedroom and I heard a car pull up outside.

Maybe it's Bryce coming to give Jesse another stolen phone? I thought and sat bolt upright. But then an even worse thought entered my mind: *What if it's the police coming to arrest Jesse?*

I held my breath and waited nervously for the sound of footsteps crunching along the drive followed by the ding of the doorbell. My fear made the colours illuminate and glow in the darkness like the Northern Lights. It was stunning, but it didn't have me feeling any less afraid that the police had come for my brother.

It was only when I heard a woman's voice say goodbye to someone and the car headlights started to drift away that I could finally breathe a sigh of relief. And once I'd slid back down into my bed, the colours began to fade, leaving the dark to swallow me up again like an enormous blanket.

I was glad it wasn't the police, but I knew the sooner that phone was out of our house, the better.

CHAPTER 41

It was hard trying to hide my worry from Mama at breakfast on Monday.

'Are you sure you're feeling OK?' she asked.

I'd hardly touched my cornflakes, just like I'd barely eaten any of her stew the previous night, and I'm sure she'd noticed.

But like I'd done yesterday over dinner, I told Mama I was fine, even though my stomach was in knots at the thought of confronting Bryce Mackenzie.

'But you don't look fine,' Mama went on. 'Actually, you look a little peaky.'

'There's nothing wrong with me. Honest, Mama. And besides, I don't want to miss school as Mrs Downing is going to be holding an art competition with the best picture winning a secret prize, and you know how I love a competition.'

Although I did have art today, there wasn't any competition. But it was the only thing I could think of to get Mama off my back. In any case, she seemed to believe me and turned her attention to my brother, who was busy stirring his spoon around his bowl of Cheerios instead of wolfing it down like he usually does.

'And what's happened to your appetite?' she asked.

If only Mama knew what was really going on. But for sure she'd go nuts.

'I'm just not that hungry,' Jesse muttered.

I knew he was as worried as I was.

'Well,' said Mama, 'I only hope you both get your appetites back by this evening, as I was planning to make chicken fajitas and a chocolate cake with ice cream for dessert.'

Hearing what Mama was doing for dinner would've normally had me fizzing with excitement, but I couldn't muster up any joy.

'So what's the plan?' I asked Jesse when Mama was out of earshot.

He shrugged. 'I figured I'd just hand the phone back to Bryce and let him know that our friendship is over. And hopefully, that'll be it and there won't be any trouble.'

'Well, if there is trouble, then I'll protect you with

my superpower,' I said, trying my best to sound confident, even though I wasn't entirely sure how I could keep Jesse safe.

My fear continued to loom as large as the colour clouds that accompanied me to school, and once my lessons began, I found it really hard to concentrate on anything.

'Are you all right, Prune?' asked Doug at the end of our English lesson, having obviously noticed something was bothering me.

'Yeah, I'm OK,' I fibbed.

But as the day progressed, I continued to worry about Jesse's predicament.

'There is something the matter, isn't there?' said Doug as we made our way to the hall for lunch, his face looking even more concerned than it had earlier.

'Yeah, there is,' I admitted finally.

I quietly told Doug everything about the phone and Jesse and how I was scared of what Bryce might do.

'And if you tell your mum—'

I shook my head because telling Mama wasn't an option as far as Jesse was concerned. 'I wish I could, Doug, but I can't.'

'Well, try not to worry, Prune,' Doug whispered sympathetically as we got our plates filled up at the serving station. 'As you said, all your brother needs to do is give the phone back.'

'It sounds simple enough, but I'm not so sure it will be,' I said as we walked and sat down at our class's table.

'Well, it's got to be simpler than … this!' said Doug. He scooped up his apple from his tray and my pear, then swiped the apples from the trays of Theo and Amber.

He started to juggle and made funny faces as he tried to bite into the fruit simultaneously. Kids wandered over to watch and before he knew it, Doug had a captive audience who whooped and clapped when he was finished, his mouth stuffed full of fruit and his face smeared with juice.

Doug seemed completely taken aback by all the attention.

'That was ace!' said Theo, not looking the slightest bit annoyed that Doug had eaten half his lunch.

'Yeah, that was really cool,' said Amber as we all looked at Doug in surprise.

'I didn't know you could juggle,' I said.

'I've not been doing it that long. Though it's actually not that difficult,' said Doug. 'I was hoping it would cheer you up, Prune.'

I smiled. 'Thank you, Doug.'

He had helped me forget my worries, if only for a little bit.

*　*　*

As the rest of the day rolled on, although I was still feeling anxious about Bryce, I started to wonder how I could repay Doug for his kindness, and not just for impressing me with his juggling skills, but for everything he'd done for me since I'd joined Maple Lane. Without Doug as my friend, things might have been a lot worse when I was having the Vile-lets to contend with.

'Doug, if you could have anything right now, what would it be?' I asked him during afternoon break.

'Having my own private jet would be great,' he answered.

'I was, um, thinking of something a little smaller.'

Doug tapped his chin as he thought about my question again. 'A big bar of chocolate would be nice.'

'Cool, maybe I can help you out with that.'

'How do you mean?'

'I'll tell you later.'

Doug glanced at me puzzled, but I simply grinned.

CHAPTER 42

My last lesson of the day was art, and when the bell rang for home time, I asked Doug to wait five minutes then come and meet me in the school library. And before he could ask why, I was already sprinting off.

Thankfully there was no one in the library, so I got out my sketchbook and started drawing a picture of a chocolate bar. I didn't need to summon the colours because they'd barely left my side the entire day due to my fear of what Bryce might do to Jesse. So as soon as I'd finished my drawing and willed the picture to be real, in a flash, a bar of chocolate measuring at least a metre long appeared on the table in front of me.

'So what did you want to see me about?' said Doug, walking in and instantly stopping in his tracks when he saw the chocolate, his mouth open wide like a tunnel. 'Where did you get that from?'

'My mama made it,' I said, making the fib up on the spot. 'She likes to make chocolate in her spare time.'

'It looks incredible, Prune,' said Doug, his blue eyes sparkling. 'But how did you even manage to get it to school?'

'I had some help,' I continued to fib.

'But how were you able to sneak in something so big?!' said Doug, looking perplexed.

'Um ...' I bit my lip.

I couldn't keep lying to Doug and nor did I want to. He'd been such a good friend, so it just didn't feel right keeping my power a secret from him.

'Actually, Doug, I've discovered something that's out-of-this-world fantastic.'

'What?' said Doug curiously.

'Theo wasn't making it up when he said there are people with superpowers.'

'Are you talking about those videos on YouTube? Because trust me, Prune, they're all fake. And as much as I'd love to believe there really are people out there with superpowers, it just isn't true.'

'Well, what if I told you I had a superpower?'

Doug looked at me oddly. 'But you don't. Nobody does.'

'I know it sounds hard to believe, but I really do have a superpower, Doug. That's how this chocolate got here. I can bring my drawings to life.'

'All right, why don't you show me?' he said, but his face remained sceptical.

'I will, but you need to promise you won't tell anybody. I'm only telling you because I feel that I can trust you, plus you've been a really good friend.'

'OK, I promise I won't tell.'

'Cool. So what would you like me to draw?'

'Um, why not some more chocolate!' said Doug.

'Sure, but I won't make it as big this time.'

I drew another bar of chocolate in my sketchbook, and once I'd started the process of bringing the picture to life, a much smaller bar of chocolate appeared on the palm of my hand.

Doug was flabbergasted. 'How did you do that?'

'I have a superpower – it's as simple as that.'

'But how long have you had it?'

'Not long …' I said.

I explained in detail, to a shocked-looking Doug, how it had all begun and how it all worked. Then I told him how Jesse and I reckoned my power might have something to do with the Delmere Magic and about what we'd found out at the library.

'So the Delmere Magic might actually be true then,'

said Doug, clearly awestruck. 'Well, I guess I take everything back about there not being any real people with superpowers. And your power, Prune, is mega fantastic. I mean, who wouldn't want to be able to bring things to life?!'

'It is great having a superpower, only it hasn't been the easiest to handle. There have been times when the things I've brought to life have gone a bit wrong,' I said frankly.

And without mentioning Fake Dad, I told Doug about the scarf, the peacock and the tiger.

'You had an actual tiger in your garden!' said Doug, blinking fast.

'Yeah, but the whole thing was completely terrifying.'

'Well, not all superheroes have it easy, Prune. Take the Hulk, for example. He can't always control his temper! Or there's the Thing from the Fantastic Four. He had to put up with looking like a messy blob of clay,' said Doug, trying in his own way to be understanding.

'Superhero or not, I am still the same person, Doug. Nothing else has changed.'

Yet the way Doug was looking at me – as though I was a mysterious person he'd just met – made me feel like something *had* changed. The truth was, I was no longer a regular kid.

'And you do mean it, don't you? That you won't tell anyone about my superpower?' I said to Doug.

I guess I just needed some extra assurance.

'Don't worry – your secret's safe with me. Anyway, a lot of superheroes keep their powers a secret.' He walked around the bar of chocolate. 'So will it just taste like normal chocolate?' said Doug, his face still astounded by it.

I nodded. 'Why don't you try a bit?'

It took Doug a good couple of minutes to break off a chunk, even with my help, the two of us trying to pull a piece off together.

'It tastes amazing!' said Doug, taking a bite. 'This is one of the best things anyone's ever done for me, Prune,' he added with a smile that seemed as enormous as the chocolate.

'We'll probably still be eating this well into next year!' said Doug's dad, as he and Doug heaved the bar of chocolate into the back seat of their car. He turned to me. 'Doug speaks very highly of you, Prune. Thanks for being a great friend to him.'

And as they drove off, I felt pleased I'd been able to use my power to perform another good deed.

I'd even managed to forget about Bryce … That was until I arrived home, when my fear and worry immediately returned, making my stomach feel sick as if I'd eaten all of Doug's chocolate.

Jesse was sat in the living room with his rucksack beside him, and he looked nervous.

'Have you got the phone?' I asked.

He nodded and tapped his rucksack. 'I even have the trainers.'

'So I guess we're ready to go then.'

Jesse looked at me thoughtfully. 'Look, Prune, maybe it's not such a good idea you coming with me. I know you want to, but I shouldn't be involving you in all this.'

'I'm already involved. But don't worry, I've got your back.'

'Since when did you become all grown up?' said Jesse. He smiled but then shook his head. 'I'm not going to be able to talk you out of this, am I?'

'Nope,' I replied, shaking my own head.

'Well, like I said last night, just make sure you stay back.'

'You are doing the right thing you know, Jesse.'

He sighed. 'I know.'

As we left the house, I tried to reassure myself that nothing bad would happen. Jesse would hand back the phone and tell Bryce he no longer wanted to be his friend. But my words weren't enough to shut off a small voice in my head that was telling me we were about to put ourselves in danger.

A danger that felt even scarier than coming face to face with an angry tiger.

CHAPTER 43

Jesse and I were quiet on our bus journey to Ocean View. He was listening to his iPod, which I suppose helped to keep him distracted. I took out my sketchbook and started to draw a picture of a helter-skelter.

'Nice picture,' said a boy sitting behind us, which made me quickly shut my sketchbook. The boy had a line shaved into his hair that looked like a lightning bolt. He had hazel-brown eyes and looked about my age.

'Thanks,' I replied shyly.

I started thinking about the time I'd been on a real helter-skelter at the funfair two years earlier. I'd enjoyed it so much that I went on it three times … I wished more than anything that I could've been back at that funfair rather than where we were heading.

The boy got off at the next stop and out of the window I noticed he'd dropped his phone. As the bus started moving, I glimpsed him turn round to pick it up. Only he didn't *pick it up*, because the phone literally shot up into his hand like when Thor summons his hammer.

I blinked in shock.

Had I just seen a kid with a superpower?

I nudged Jesse. 'Did you see that?'

'See what?' he said, taking out his earphones. But it was clear he'd been too engrossed in his music to have seen anything.

'The boy who was sitting behind us … he had a superpower! At least I think he did.'

'Really? How do you know?' said Jesse.

Truthfully I couldn't be completely sure that the boy did have a superpower. Still, I told Jesse what I saw.

'Well, maybe you'll get to see him again and you'll be able to find out for certain if he does have a superpower,' said Jesse.

'Hopefully,' I replied, smiling at the thought of getting to meet a fellow superhuman.

'Bryce said he'd meet me at the basketball court,' said Jesse, standing up to ring the bell as we pulled into Ocean View.

We got off the bus and began to walk down our old high street. It was nice to see some familiar places such as Bella's Cupcakes, the hairdresser Mama used to go to, and our favourite Chinese takeaway, the Golden Dragon, which did amazing spring rolls.

When we reached Shellwood Park, we headed straight for the basketball court but found it deserted. Usually, at that time of day, I would've expected to see some kids in there playing a game, so I instantly felt on edge. I breathed in the air like a cup of hot chocolate, only its warmth wasn't enough to ease my churning stomach or the colour clouds encircling me.

'Maybe we should go home,' I said to Jesse.

'We can't,' he responded. 'I told Bryce to meet me here, and he'll be raging if I bomb out – and anyway, I thought you wanted me to give him the phone back.'

'I do … but …' I sighed, knowing we couldn't afford to chicken out.

So much for trying to be a superhero.

After just a minute of standing on an empty basketball court, I was already running scared.

'OK, we'll just wait for him to come,' I relented, chewing my lip in trepidation.

Five minutes later, Bryce and Zack strolled in, their footsteps echoing around us.

'Hey, guys,' said Jesse, stuffing his hands in his pockets.

'So what's happening, Jesse?' said Bryce. 'What did you want to see me about?'

'Why is your little sister here?' said Zack, looking directly at me. 'Are you babysitting or something?'

And both he and Bryce laughed.

'Yeah, kind of …' said Jesse before motioning at me to stand back.

'So are you taking care of *things* like I asked?' said Bryce. 'You did say I could count on you. I hope you meant it.'

'That's actually what I wanted to see you about …' Jesse took a breath. 'Look, Bryce, I don't know why you wanted me to take care of *the phone*, but … I um …'

'Just spit it out,' said Bryce.

'I um … came here to give it back and to say that I'm not going to be doing anything like this for you again. So don't ask me to and don't come looking for me. We're done, all right?'

For the longest minute, there was an eerie quietness as Bryce and Zack stared at Jesse, not saying a word. Then they burst out laughing again.

'Zack, are you hearing this?' said Bryce, putting his hands behind his head. 'Looks like Jesse doesn't want to be our friend any more.'

Bryce's lips turned down in mock sadness.

'I think he's taking the mickey, Bryce,' said Zack as my heart started to race.

'I'm not. I'm being serious,' said Jesse, and although

his voice was shaky, it was defiant.

Jesse shrugged off his rucksack and pulled out the phone and the trainers. He put the trainers on the ground and held the phone out to Bryce.

'Here, take it.'

Bryce took the phone.

Well, that was easy, I thought, and just as I was about to say, 'Can we go now, Jesse?' Bryce said, 'Nah, I don't want this back, not yet. I asked you to take care of it, and taking care of it is what you're going to do.'

Bravely, Jesse shook his head. 'I'm sorry, Bryce, I can't do that.'

Bryce shrugged. 'That's not how things work around here, Jesse – you know that. Because when me and my boys ask you to do something, you do it, no questions.'

'He doesn't want the phone!' I yelled, but this only made Bryce and Zack laugh some more.

'Whoa, little girl!' said Bryce then glanced back at Jesse. 'Now why didn't you tell me you were bringing Prune as backup?'

Jesse spun round and narrowed his eyes at me.

'*Sorry*,' I mouthed, hoping I hadn't gone and made things worse.

'But it looks like Prune has got more guts than you,' Bryce quipped. 'Maybe she'd be a better friend to us.'

'I don't want to be your friend, not ever!' I said sharply.

'It's all right. We've got enough friends already,' said Zack, 'and they no longer include *this* wimp.' He looked at my brother in disgust.

Bryce held out the phone to Jesse. 'Take it back.'

'No, I'm not going to do that,' said Jesse.

'OK,' said Bryce, putting the phone in the back pocket of his jeans. He cracked his knuckles as he and Zack stood right up close to Jesse. 'Just who do you think you are, coming here trying to disrespect us?'

'I'm not,' said Jesse.

Bryce snorted. 'Grab him, Zack!'

Suddenly Zack had my brother by the arm and was twisting it.

'Get off!' shouted Jesse.

I was petrified, but I knew I had to stop them.

'You let him go right now!' I shrieked.

'Keep out of this, Prune!' said Bryce as he shoved my brother. 'It has nothing to do with you.'

In that moment I knew I had to do something. I quickly got out my sketchbook and pencils and started to draw, panic rushing through me. I was drawing so fast that I wasn't even sure what I was drawing.

'Please, Bryce, I didn't come here to fight,' said Jesse.

'That's because you're a coward!' Bryce shouted then punched Jesse straight in the stomach.

'Stop!' I screamed as Jesse yowled in agony.

But Bryce and Zack took no notice.

'When I ask you to do something, you do it or pay the price. I thought you of all people knew that,' said Bryce as he shoved my brother again, making him fall to the ground.

Tears pricked my eyes as I willed my picture to come to life, knowing my fear was all that the colours needed to make it happen. Within an instant, a huge gust of wind blew around us, and in the corner of the court a large spinning funnel appeared.

'That's a … that's a … *tornado!*' said Bryce, the wind feeling like a thousand hair dryers blowing on to our faces.

'And it's coming to get you!' I yelled at him.

'No, it can't be a tornado – it can't be!' Bryce squealed. 'We don't get tornados in this town.'

But the tornado was inching closer.

'Well, whether it is or isn't a tornado,' said Zack, looking terrified, 'I think it's best we get out of here before we end up inside it!'

And I've never seen two people run so fast, their bodies blurring into one as they fled from the court.

I ran over to Jesse and helped him up.

'Are you OK?'

'Yeah, I'm fine, but we need to get out of here too, Prune,' he said, looking across at the tornado, which was still spinning wildly.

I hastily tried to imagine the tornado disappearing, but nothing happened – in fact it was now heading towards us!

'Let's go!' said Jesse as he grabbed my hand.

And we ran as fast as we could, the tornado chasing us down like a monster in a scary film.

'Quick – down here!' said Jesse, and we slipped down an alleyway.

'You've got to make it disappear, Prune!' he panted.

'I'm trying to,' I whimpered, only my head felt so jumbled that I couldn't get my mind to concentrate.

Car alarms began to blare as the lamp post in the alleyway shook like a twig. A rubbish bin careened towards us like a bowling ball.

'Watch out!' said Jesse, pulling me out of its way before it went crashing into a garage door at the end of the alleyway.

I frantically tried to get my mind to be quiet so I could think. Only, I couldn't think! Meanwhile, the wind around us was getting stronger and stronger.

'C'mon, Prune – what's taking you so long?! Why aren't you making that tornado vanish?' said Jesse urgently.

'My power ... it's not working. I can't concentrate!'

We could now hear screaming from people who I imagined were desperately trying to get away from the tornado.

'What do you mean it's not working?!' said Jesse.

'I-I-I ... I don't know what to do!' I cried, tears pouring from my eyes. 'My power's useless!'

'Look at me, Prune,' said Jesse, clutching my shoulders.

I wiped my tears with my hands as I looked up at him.

'Your power is *not* useless – it's amazing, and *you're amazing*. You're the best sister anyone could have and I believe in you, Prune. You've got this, OK?'

'But I can't stop it, Jesse!' I sobbed.

'Yes, you can, Prune. Just try and focus.'

With trepidation, I looked over at the approaching tornado, and it was as if it had been hunting us down, because now it was at the top of the alleyway, and it was even *bigger*.

I gulped.

'I'm not sure I can focus, Jesse. I'm too scared!'

'Don't be scared, Prune,' he said and gave me a quick cuddle. 'Maybe you just need to think of some-thing that will help you focus,' he added as the tornado howled like a hungry wolf.

'Like what?'

'Um … maybe something that makes you feel happy.'

Our clothes billowed and we could barely stand, but we had no way of escaping.

'Think of something happy? But what if that doesn't work?' I shouted through the wind, trying to hold on as tightly as I could to Jesse's hand.

'You just have to try, Prune!' he yelled, the tornado dragging us towards it.

We were about to get sucked up!

I immediately thought of how much I loved Jesse and how wonderful it was to have him as my brother, and I let that happy thought wrap itself around me like a hug. My mind felt clear for the first time since the colours first appeared, since Grandma Jean had died, and with my eyes closed, I imagined the tornado disappearing. Then, a moment later, it had vanished and everything was calm once more.

'You did it, Prune! You did it!' said Jesse, cuddling me again.

I felt so relieved.

'Wowsers!' I murmured. 'That tornado could've done some serious damage.'

'Well, it's gone now and that's all that matters,' said Jesse.

'Your idea worked, you know. Thinking of a happy thought helped me to focus.'

My brother smiled. 'That's good.'

I had a thought. 'Maybe this means when I summon the colours in the future, I won't need to connect with any sad feelings to make them appear. Maybe I can do it by focusing on happy feelings instead.'

'So have you never tried that before?' asked Jesse.

I shook my head.

'Well, I guess you'll only know for sure if that works the next time you bring another picture to life. But just make sure it's not another tornado,' said Jesse, smiling. 'Thank you, Prune, for helping me out today. I should've realised you're someone I can rely on. And who would've thought it? My little sister, a real-life superhero who's also the best sister ever!'

I smiled back, a feeling of pride blooming through me.

For the first time, I'd got to use my power to help somebody who really needed it – who had nowhere else to turn. We might not have totally defeated the bad guys, but we'd bought ourselves some time. And even though I might not wear a cape, just being there for my big brother felt pretty super.

CHAPTER 44

Almost a week had passed since that day in the basket-ball court, and while Jesse and I had spent most of it worrying if Bryce would be looking for revenge, we hadn't heard a peep out of him since he and Zack had run from the tornado. Then finally Jesse found out from someone else that both Bryce and Zack had got themselves arrested and charged after getting caught with several stolen phones in Bryce's car.

'I think that tornado properly scared Bryce and Zack,' said Jesse as we stood in the kitchen making peach cobbler together on Saturday evening. 'But I expect getting arrested felt even scarier.' He sighed. 'I know it was bound to happen at some point, but at least it means now I won't have Bryce pushing me around.'

'But you do know it would've been you who'd got arrested had you not given the phone back?' I said.

Jesse nodded. 'I know.'

'And you are definitely done with Bryce? You won't start hanging out with him again if he gets in touch?'

'Yeah, I'm done with him. No going back.'

It had been Jesse's idea to make peach cobbler for dessert, using Grandma's recipe. But I think Jesse was doing his best to prove to Mama that he was a changed person in more ways than one. He was managing to do all his chores and had told both me and Mama that he'd never skip school again, assuring us he meant it this time. And tonight was movie night. Well, that's what Mama had decided to call it after we had a new smart TV delivered earlier in the day.

Jesse had wanted me to draw us a TV to save Mama the expense of buying one, but Mama insisted on getting it without my help. But the thing she did want me to help her with was choosing a film to watch. I decided on *Captain Marvel*. And even though I'd already seen it heaps of times, I was excited to watch it again because it's such a great film. But what I did make real was a very large bowl of popcorn and a tub of ice cream to go with the peach cobbler.

And the best part of all was I was able to summon the colours by focusing on happy feelings, which danced in my tummy like a kite in the sky. Feelings that came from all the wonderful moments I'd enjoyed in my life, from laughing at Jesse's jokes to enjoying Mama's cuddles, and having sleepovers with Corinne to winning prizes for my drawings.

'I have to say, this has surely been an interesting few weeks,' said Mama as she sat in between me and Jesse, the three of us all huddled on the sofa with Grandma's quilt spread over us. 'And I still can't get over the fact that my little girl has a superpower.'

'Oh, it's no big deal,' I said, playing it down.

'No big deal?' said Jesse. 'Course it's a big deal.'

'What I mean is, it's just a part of who I am – isn't that right, Mama?'

She nodded. 'Yes it is.'

'Well, I think I might've developed an amazing power of my own,' said Jesse, which made Mama almost choke on her popcorn. 'I'm only kidding, but I am finally enjoying my new school, so I guess you could say that's amazing.'

'Yes, it certainly is,' said Mama, once she'd stopped coughing. 'And I can't tell you how glad that makes me, Jesse.'

He smiled. 'And a place has come up on the basketball team. They're going to let me try out next week.'

'That's great, Jesse!' said me and Mama together.

'You'll also be pleased to hear I've made friends with a couple of boys from my computer club.'

'Oh, I am pleased to hear that,' Mama replied.

'And like I said, you'll never have to worry about me bunking off school again because I'm a changed man, Mama.'

'Well, you're not a man yet, but I am proud of you, son,' said Mama, cupping his face. 'In fact, I'm proud of the both of you,' she added, putting her arms around us. 'And, Prune, I hope there'll come a time when you can let the whole world know about your power and you won't have to keep it a secret.'

'But you will still let me use it?' I asked.

'Yes, so long as you're able to use it in a way that means the world doesn't find out just yet,' said Mama.

'So, if Prune wanted to bring to life a pet, would she be able to?' asked Jesse, looking hopeful.

'I hope you're not thinking about another tiger,' said Mama.

'Actually, I was thinking about a dog,' said Jesse.

'Yeah, I'd love to have a dog!' I exclaimed. 'Could we have a dog, Mama, please?'

'Maybe, but I will need to think about it,' she answered, mulling it over.

'Actually, I wouldn't want to draw a dog and bring it to life,' I said. 'So perhaps we could get a real dog from a rescue centre instead?'

'That sounds like a sensible idea,' said Mama. 'You're always so considerate, Prune.' She paused for a moment. 'Do you know what? I think getting a dog would be just perfect.'

'*Yes!*' said Jesse.

'Awesome!' I replied.

'So, seeing as we're about to watch a film about a superhero,' said Jesse, 'have you had any more thoughts, sis, on the superhero name you'd want to give yourself?'

'I have thought of a name as it happens,' I said as he and Mama looked at me in anticipation.

I rose to my feet, a big smile on my face.

'I've decided my name will be the Wondrous Prune.'

So there you have it. That's how the events of a perfectly normal Sunday changed my life forever and how I went from being an ordinary eleven-year-old girl to becoming the Wondrous Prune!

ACKNOWLEDGEMENTS

I first want to start by thanking my late mother. Thank you for inspiring my love of words from an early age and thank you for all the books that you filled my life with. You always knew I wanted to become an author and I'll remain eternally grateful for the encouragement and support you gave me, and the sacrifices you made along the way. Although you didn't get to see my story eventually become this book, I know it meant a lot to you. Mum, you'll forever be in my heart.

A huge thank you to my fantastic agent, Rachel Mann, for your wondrous support, expertise and guidance throughout the journey of this book. A big thanks also to Zöe Griffiths, my brilliant editor, for championing this story and helping me to develop it and perfect the voice of

Prune. I'm extremely grateful. Thank you to the rest of the wonderful team at Bloomsbury – Fliss Stevens, Emily Marples, Jade Westwood and Jet Purdie – and thank you to Veronica Lyons for doing such a superb copy-edit.

I fell in love with the cover of *The Wondrous Prune* from the moment I saw it. Thank you so, so much, Chaaya Prabhat, for your beautiful illustration, which captures the essence of Prune's power.

Thank you to Catherine Campbell for your wisdom and encouragement, and Loretta Allen and Irene Greenwood for always lending an ear on those lunchtime walks we have. Thank you to Lisa Chavda and Dinah Brown for all your support too. And, finally, much love and thanks to my family.

Q&A WITH ELLIE CLEMENTS

1. *The Wondrous Prune* is such a fantastic book. Did you always want to be a writer? How did you begin?

Yes, I have wanted to be a writer ever since I was a child. I always enjoyed writing short stories, and that continued as I grew up, until one day I decided to write a full-length novel.

2. *The Wondrous Prune* is about a girl who discovers that she has an extraordinary power. Have you always been interested in superheroes? What did you find exciting when writing about Prune's magical ability?

I've been a long-time fan of superheroes, with my favourites being Storm from the X-Men, and Superman.

I've loved all the X-Men and Superman films that have been made. Other favourites of mine include The Avengers and the Spider-Man films.

I love how Prune's ability is simply out of this world. She has the power to bring anything to life through her drawings, and that meant I could have a lot of fun thinking up the most brilliant things to include.

3. Even though Prune's life becomes extraordinary, she still has to cope with everyday struggles. How important was it to you to bring alive that reality for readers?

It was very important to me that the book reflected the realities that some children face, such as bullying or dealing with the upheavals of moving to a new town or city, and I think showing the challenges that Prune goes through makes her more relatable as a character.

Throughout the book we also see how Prune gains a better understanding of her feelings, which is all part of growing up, and in the story Prune's emotions are expressed through the amazing and abundant colours she sees.

4. What kind of books do you like to read?

I like to read a range of different books. I particularly like mysteries and stories that make me laugh. Plus it's always great to read a story that has a rich array of interesting and engaging characters.

5.   What is your next book about?

It's about a boy called Sonny, who – like Prune – has an amazing superpower. However, his is that he can move objects with his mind! But like Prune's power, Sonny's can be a bit hit-and-miss sometimes. You might notice that Sonny makes a brief appearance in *The Wondrous Prune*.

6.   What do you like to do when you're not writing?

I enjoy going on long walks and going to art galleries, because I love art even though, unlike Prune, I'm hopeless at drawing! I also enjoy singing, and never miss the opportunity to belt out a song whenever there's a karaoke machine around.

LOOK OUT FOR

THE
STUPENDOUS
SONNY

COMING SOON!

ABOUT THE AUTHOR

Ellie Clements was born in London and decided she wanted to become an author at the age of nine, when her favourite hobby was writing short stories. Her passion for writing continued and she later studied journalism at university. Ellie's working life has mostly been spent in the charity sector, and when she isn't busy writing for children, she enjoys long walks, browsing her local bookshop and the occasional spot of karaoke.